THINK
OF
LAURA

ALSO BY FRANK ZAFIRO

<u>Stefan Kopriva Mysteries</u>
Waist Deep
Lovely, Dark and Deep
Friend of the Departed
Hope Dies Last
Think of Laura
The Sins of Somebody Else's Past (*)

<u>River City Series</u>
Under a Raging Moon
Heroes Often Fail
Beneath a Weeping Sky
And Every Man Has To Die
The Menace of the Years
Place of Wrath and Tears
Dirty Little Town
Dead Even (short stories)
Some Degree of Murder
No Good Deed (short stories)
The Worst Kind of Truth
Chisolm's Debt
The Cleaner (short stories)
All the Forgotten Yesterdays
Nor Shadowed Heart (*)
The Trade Off
Sugar Got Low (short stories)

SpoCompton Crime Novels
Bricks & Cam Jobs (with Eric Beetner)
Charlie-316 series (with Colin Conway)
The Ania Series (with Jim Wilsky)
Jack McCrae Mysteries
Sandy Banks Thrillers

THINK OF LAURA

A STEFAN KOPRIVA NOVEL

BY

FRANK ZAFIRO

THINK OF LAURA: A STEFAN KOPRIVA NOVEL (#5)

By Frank Zafiro

© 2024 by Frank Scalise

Code 4 Press, an imprint of Frank Zafiro, LLC
Redmond, Oregon USA

This is a work of fiction. While real locations may be used to add authenticity to the story, all characters appearing in this book are fictitious. Any resemblance to real persons, living or dead, is purely coincidental.

Cover Design by Eric Beetner

ISBN: 978-1-962889-06-3

For everyone who has known desperate moments and regret.

A sea of people
A sea of masks
Worn out of fear
Need
To complete simple tasks.

Obscuring truth
Causing strife
Shielding sadness
Hiding a secret life.

Our masks save us.
Our masks strangle us.

—Rebecca Battaglia

1

"Will you find my sister?" a tearful Missy Jardin asked me.

We were in my employer's office. Missy stared out from beneath long eyelashes, clutching a tissue and dabbing at her eyes. Her face was round, almost cherub-like except for full, pouting lips. Her blond hair hung well past her shoulders. The way it damn near gleamed spoke to how much care and attention she must have paid to those golden tresses. Her white dress was fringed with blue. Even though she was seated when I'd entered the room, her curves were easy enough to see.

She was an attractive woman, no doubt.

I didn't like her at all.

This reaction wasn't necessarily an uncommon one in this job. Working for a defense attorney, even an honorable one like Joel Harrity, resulted in frequent instances in which I haven't particularly liked the client he was representing. Whether this was some remnant of my world-view from when I was still a cop—now closing in on sixteen years ago—or the result of my ongoing relationship with one, I couldn't say.

I was equally hard-pressed to say why Missy

1

rubbed me wrong from the first moment I met her. Her emotion certainly seemed genuine. Even so, I sensed some underlying deception within her. It was a gut reaction, true. But I'd learned to pay heed to my gut when it tries to warn me. The reaction might not be infallible, but it was right often enough to warrant examination.

Either way, my opinion of her was largely irrelevant. Harrity chose his clients and I worked for Harrity.

When I didn't answer her question about finding her sister, it was Harrity who stepped in. The tall, slender lawyer spoke in the self-assured tone I'd seen calm many a client. "We can't promise results, Miss Jardin," he said, "but my investigator is very good, and I can promise he'll make every effort to find Laura."

Harrity's compliment wasn't lost on me. He wasn't a man to offer them often, so I took a moment to enjoy the pat on the back while I settled into the chair opposite Missy.

"I need to get up to speed here," I said. I glanced at Harrity, but his gaze flicked to Missy. Clearly, he was going to let me get the information from her in the order I preferred. "Tell me why you're here."

Missy dabbed her eyes again. "I thought I might need a lawyer."

"Why?"

"I don't know for sure. Dania said so."

"Dania?"

"My friend. I work with her."

I glanced up at Harrity and mimed a writing motion. Wordlessly, the attorney dug a legal pad out of his desk and handed it to me, along with a pen. The heft of his writing instrument felt foreign in my hand. I was used to the much cheaper, disposable ones.

"What's Dania's last name?" I asked Missy.

"Miller."

"Where do you two work?"

"Kitty's Koffee Korner."

The pen rolled smoothly across the paper as I jotted down the information. "Why did Dania say you needed a lawyer?"

"To protect my rights?" Missy sounded confused when she spoke the words.

I glanced up at her. "Your rights? Have you been arrested for something?"

"What? No." She shook her head. "My sister, Laura, is missing. I'm her only family. Except for Erik, of course."

"And Erik is…?"

"Her husband. Erik Shelton."

I wrote down Erik's name. "So… what rights are you concerned about?"

"I'm not sure," she admitted. "Dania said if Laura is…" She let out a small sob and put the tissue to her face again.

I waited for her to regain her composure. Over the course of my few years as a cop, I quickly learned offering consolation is counter-productive. Instead, I let the person work through the moment.

Missy took a little while to do so. She cast a single furtive glance up at me, as if inviting me to comfort her. That glance told me something about her. There was an on-stage quality to her persona. Her reaction was an overly dramatic reaction to a genuine emotional response. It reminded me of how people behaved on the so-called reality shows that were becoming all the rage.

I couldn't stomach those shows, even though my girlfriend watched them for escape. I complained to Anna that everyone was either faking it or overreacting.

"That's the point," she assured me. "It's the entire allure, in fact."

I didn't understand it. Given what I knew she encountered each night on patrol, reality TV seemed like it would be a busman's holiday for her. She told me why it wasn't.

"I don't have to solve the situation," Anna explained. "I can just rubberneck like everyone else."

The idea still didn't appeal to me. In my role as an investigator for Harrity, I came across enough drama and deception. I didn't want to experience more of it for entertainment purposes. So, Anna and I crossed reality TV off our joint viewing slate.

Missy reminded me of those shows. But there was another element that was becoming clear to me the more she spoke. A sense of entitlement lurked underneath her exterior, as well. I suspected this was learned behavior, something I saw in celebrities, powerful figures, or simply in beautiful people. The last certainly applied to Missy. I imagined she was used to people deferring to her, scrambling to open doors, or doing favors, hoping for a smile or other attention.

I waited without moving or saying a word.

Finally, Missy regained her composure. Then she said, "If something bad has happened to her… if she's gone, then Dania said I needed to protect my rights as a sister."

I rested the pen on the notepad. "I'm confused. Your sister is missing?"

Missy nodded. "For almost two weeks now."

"Are the police involved?"

"Yes."

"What do they say?"

"The detective won't talk to me, only Erik. Erik said they can't find her."

"That's why you're here?"

She nodded again.

I glanced at Harrity again. Now, I wished I'd let him give me a summary at the start. Missy wasn't making any sense. If she wanted to find her sister and didn't think the police were doing a good job, why didn't she go to a private investigator? River City had plenty of those and all of them licensed, something I wasn't.

Harrity read my expression and stepped in. "Miss Jardin's colleague convinced her she needed to examine her standing in the event her sister's disappearance becomes permanent," he said.

"Upon speaking with her, however, it has become clear that her primary concern is locating Laura Shelton."

"We're not going to refer her to a PI firm?"

"Not yet," Harrity said. "She may yet require representation."

"Why?"

"As she stated, her interests in her sister's estate."

I thought about that for a moment, then turned back to Missy. "Are you saying her husband is a suspect in her disappearance?"

Tears welled up in her eyes once more. "I don't want to think so. But for her to just disappear, with no word to me or anyone else? It's unlike her."

"Were you two close?"

Missy bobbed her head. "God, yes. Ever since we were kids." She dabbed at her eyes and let out a wavering breath. "Our mom was an alcoholic and Dad was never around, so she always took care of me."

"How much older than you is she?"

"Nine years."

"That's a lot," I noted.

"Is it?" She shrugged. "I don't have anything to compare it to. All my life, Laura has taken care of me, even when I stopped needing it."

"What do you mean?"

"Just that she was protective. She looked out for me when it came to boyfriends or my bosses." She smiled sadly. "Whenever we went out for drinks or lunch, she always paid, no matter what. She said that's what big sisters were for. I didn't even try to pick up the check."

"Is Laura well off?" I asked.

Missy's gaze cut to Harrity, then back to me. "Not exactly."

2

After Missy Jardin departed, Harrity explained more completely.

"Laura Shelton was recently accused of embezzling funds from her employer, Lawrence Pines. Pines is the owner of a small cleaning business, Fresh Pines. Laura is—or *was*— the bookkeeper."

I rubbed my chin, thinking. The remainder of Missy Jardin's interview had consisted of more tears and, eventually, an inability to continue. She apologized profusely and left, pausing only to get assurances from Harrity that his help—and mine— was forthcoming.

"I'm a little confused," I admitted. "Is Laura Shelton a fugitive or a missing person?"

"Her exact status is unclear. Officially, the police consider her missing. But it wouldn't surprise me if the detective eventually seeks an arrest warrant for her embezzlement."

"That's what I don't get," I said. "I understand you representing Laura as a defendant but her sister hasn't committed a crime."

"My caseload isn't strictly criminal," Harrity reminded me. "I take on civil matters as well."

"What's the civil case here? I mean, what does Missy Jardin have to worry about?"

"She told you that. She's concerned about her own standing in Laura Shelton's estate."

"I'm no lawyer but doesn't someone have to be dead for that to be an issue?"

"I believe that is Miss Jardin's true concern — her sister's welfare."

"That makes more sense. But that's a job for an investigative agency. It's not a legal problem."

"Nonetheless," Harrity said, "she came here and she is the client. Her legal considerations may eventually prove minimal, but I am not going to turn away someone in need." He cocked his head. "And fortunately for me, I have an investigator on retainer."

I frowned. I liked working for Harrity but this was different than most of the tasks he set me on. "I don't like it," I muttered, "and I don't like her."

Harrity was unmoved. "Liking one's clients is not a requirement in this field. If anything, doing so is a hindrance to objectivity. As for the work at hand..." He shrugged. "I can contract it out if you'd like to pass."

"No," I said. I'd become his primary investigator, working essentially full time for him. Technically, I was an independent contractor but he was *my* sole client. Turning away work from him wasn't a habit I wanted to start. Harrity wasn't petty but he was results driven. I didn't need someone else supplanting my role as his go-to investigator. "I'll do it. Just tell me what you need."

"Let's keep matters simple. Find Laura Shelton."

My frown deepened. One thing I felt certain about was that this case was *not* going to be simple.

"Sure thing," I told Harrity, forcing some enthusiasm into my tone. "I'm on it."

3

I waited around Harrity's office for a few minutes while his assistant, Kylie, burned a copy of the case file for me. Once she handed the thin folder to me, I said, "Can you make a request for the police report?"

"Sure," she said. "But I'll have to do a public request, since it isn't discovery for a defendant client."

"That's fine."

She gave me an indulgent smile. "That means the report will be redacted."

"Oh," I said, realizing her point. Anything with a privacy element attached to it would be blacked out. Other sensitive information might be, too, and figuring out what was underneath could be difficult without context. Still, it was better than nothing. "Can you get the name of the investigating detective first? Maybe he'll play nice. If not, we'll go with the public request."

"Sure," said Kylie.

I thanked her and left.

My car was parked almost two blocks away.

Harrity's office was located near the courthouse which was a desirable location for a defense attorney but made finding parking spaces difficult. As I trudged along in the slightly hitching gait caused by my prosthetic, I tried to push past my misgivings.

Part of being professional was to simply do whatever job is placed in front of you. I'd been doing investigations for Harrity for several years now, even surpassing my brief tenure as a police officer. While my time on the job ended in ignominy, I'd found success in this new role. It wasn't one my former peers respected but I didn't care much about what they thought of me. That ship had sailed long ago. Anna was the only person who both wore a badge and whose opinion mattered to me.

Did I reach a point of being a true professional in the four years I spent as a cop?

If someone had asked me during that time, I wouldn't have hesitated to answer yes. Looking back, though, I saw how brash I was. How I took unnecessary risks and let my emotions drive my decisions. Especially anger.

I knew I was different now. But given my reaction to this case, maybe not as professional as I thought.

"Doesn't matter," I murmured to myself. All that mattered was getting the job done.

I slipped my keys into the door of my aged Celica. I eased myself into the driver's seat, taking extra care with the prosthetic that made up the lower part of my left leg. Then I buckled in and turned the ignition. The starter groaned a little before the engine caught. I put the car into gear and headed out to find Laura Shelton.

4

My first stop on that journey was Erik Shelton. Talking to Laura's husband was the most obvious move and had the most potential to bear fruit. For one thing, if Laura had been killed, he was the most likely suspect. Also, if she were missing or on the run, Erik might not know where she was but he'd have the kind of information that might help me find her.

Actually, I realized Erik wasn't the best source of information available to me. That would be the detective who was assigned to the case. My own aversion to interacting with law enforcement came into play and I decided to delay that conversation until I had a better lay of the land. For that, Erik would be helpful.

I stopped by the car dealership where he worked. According to the file, Erik was on the sales team. When I walked in well before lunch, the place was nearly empty. A perky blonde around nineteen years old sat at an over-sized, U-shaped desk near the entrance. "Welcome to Phillips Auto," she chirped cheerfully. "How can I help you?"

I glanced down at the name plaque on the desk. "Hello, Carissa. Is Erik around?"

Her smile faltered slightly. "Mr. Shelton isn't here at the moment."

"When will he be back?"

"He actually took a personal day," she said. She glanced around self-consciously, rubbing her hands on the front of her skirt. "Uh, is there someone else on the sales team I can put you with?"

"No, thanks." I smiled at her and left.

The Shelton home was a modest split-level in the Shiloh Hills neighborhood on the far north side of River City. The exterior looked recently painted, light blue with off-white accents. The driveway was empty but there was a garage, so I had no way of knowing if Erik was home or not.

Except, of course, to knock on the door.

It took a while, but eventually I heard the deadbolt latch turn and the door opened.

Erik Shelton was of average height with rugged good looks that could have landed him support roles on television. His build was solidly athletic. He kept his jet-black hair on the short side, cut just long enough to allow that purposeful messiness that had been trendy for the last few years. Even the stubble on his square-jawed face looked stylish.

He regarded me with suspicious eyes. "Who are you?"

"My name is Stefan Kopriva. I work for Joel

Harrity."

His eyes narrowed. "I've heard that name."

"Probably. He's the best defense attorney in the city."

Recognition came into his eyes. "That's right. I've seen his picture on the bus stop benches." Then his suspicion returned. His gaze swept up and down, taking me in. "What do you want?"

"I've been asked to help find your wife," I told him.

"By who? I didn't—"

"His client is Missy Jardin."

Erik Shelton closed his eyes and sighed. "Goddamnit," he muttered. "I told her to let the cops handle it."

I didn't reply to that. Instead, I waited until he'd opened his eyes again. Then I asked, "Do you think we could talk inside?"

Erik sighed again but he pushed the door wider. "Sure, why not. No putting the toothpaste back in the tube, right?"

I stepped inside the house. Erik closed the door behind me and led me up the stairs to the living room.

The interior of the house had the look of a place that was usually clean and orderly, but a few messes dotted each room we passed through. The living room had a pizza box and several beer bottles on the coffee table, plus some clothes thrown over one chair. Dishes filled one sink in the kitchen and takeout boxes were stacked precariously on the top of the kitchen garbage can. Our destination, the dining room, was less cluttered. Only a hockey bag sat on the floor. A pair of hockey sticks leaned against a chair back.

"Have a seat," Erik offered. He settled into the chair at the head of the table.

I took the one kitty-corner to him. When I placed my steno pad on the table and flipped it open, Erik held up a hand.

"Hold on a sec. What exactly did Missy hire you to do?"

"Find Laura," I said simply.

"So, you're a P.I.?"

"I'm an investigator," I said. "I work for Joel Harrity."

"But he's a lawyer."

"He is."

Erik turned up his hands. "Why does Missy need a lawyer?"

I opened my mouth to give my pat answer—that I couldn't say and it was between the client and Harrity anyway—but paused. I wanted Erik's cooperation. Maybe showing him a little trust right out of the gate would help facilitate that.

"I think maybe she got some bad advice from a co-worker," I said.

Erik snorted. "You mean Dania. That nosy bitch."

I didn't confirm his guess. "Either way, once she was in the office, Mr. Harrity determined her largest concern was finding Laura. That's what I've been asked to do."

"The cops are already on it," he said.

"Have they found her?"

His eyes narrowed slightly. "No," he admitted. "You're somehow better at it than them?"

"My role isn't to replace their investigation, just to augment it."

"Like working together?"

I shrugged. "Like both of us working toward the same goal."

Erik pursed his lips and nodded slowly. "Okay." He took a deep breath and let it out. "Honestly, I should be happy for any help at all. I'm worried sick about her."

His words had the ring of false sincerity to them, but perhaps that was simply the wear and tear of the situation. I watched him carefully as I said, "I imagine it's been difficult."

Erik chuckled ruefully. "It's been hell. First, she gets accused of some bullshit at work and then she runs off?" He shook his head, a pained expression on his face. "It's taken the wind right out of me."

"Can I ask you a few questions? I want to get a better idea of the situation."

"The situation is my wife took off and I have no idea where she is."

"When did you see her last?"

Erik leaned back and looked at the ceiling. "I've been through all this with the cops already."

"I'll get a copy of the report, but that'll take some time so anything you can tell me now would really help."

Erik let loose another sigh. "Fine." He thought some more, then said, "Today's Tuesday. Last time I saw her was the Friday before last. So, what's that, nine days? Ten?"

I made a note on my pad. "On Friday, what time was that?"

"Around six or so."

"Are you pretty certain on the time?"

He nodded. "I have a seven o'clock game every Friday." He motioned toward the equipment bag and hockey sticks at the other end of the table. "We were arguing and I cut it short to go play."

"Not a serious argument, then?"

"Not serious enough to miss my ice time over," he said. Then he frowned. "I mean, if I'd known she was going to take off, I'd have stayed and hashed it out."

"What was it about?"

He eyed me for a moment, cocking his head. "You married?"

I held up my left hand to show him my bare ring finger. He glanced at it, then back at me.

"If you were married," he said, "then you'd know."

"Know what?"

"That when you fight, what you're fighting about is never what you're fighting about."

"So, what were you really fighting about?"

"She got caught stealing money from work," Erik said. "At least, that's what *I* was fighting about.

With women, who knows?"

"You knew about the embezzlement?"

"I figured it out around the same time her boss must have."

"How'd he find out?"

"No clue. I've only ever talked to the guy a couple of times. Company Christmas parties and summer picnics, that sort of thing."

"All right. How did you figure it out, then?"

"I noticed things appearing without any charges on the credit card. I actually thought she was shoplifting at first."

"What kind of things?"

"Expensive perfume, for one. Shoes." He touched the flat, wide gold chain around his neck. "This, too. I mean, we bought each other presents the first year or so, but that stopped before we hit thirty. Then a couple of years ago, she'd spring something on me like this every once in a while. 'Just because,' she'd say." He fingered the metal. "It was kinda nice, you know? At least until I figured it all out."

"Did you consider going to the police?"

"Why? When I confronted her about it, she said the cops already knew."

"Did that turn out to be true?"

"Sure seems like it. They came to see me after she took off."

I put down my pen and folded my hands over the notepad. "What was that conversation like?" I asked. "When you confronted her?"

"I was mad, of course. I think I was relieved, too, in a strange way."

"How so?"

He glanced away. "When I smelled the new perfume, I thought maybe she got it because she was fooling around."

"Was she?" I asked, keeping my words as flat as I could for what was always a loaded question.

Erik didn't react, though. "I don't know, actually. The money became the bigger deal, is all." He shook his head. "I told her she was stupid to take it and needed to make it right."

"So she could avoid going to jail?"

"Goddamn right," Erik said. "Also to protect us."

"From?"

Erik tapped his chest. "We're married. Washington is a community property state. That means if Old Man Pines goes after her in court, I'm on the hook as much as she is. We're talking lawsuits, losing the house, garnishing my paycheck." He shook his head ruefully. "It could get ugly, man. That's why I told her to give it back."

"Was she willing to do that?"

"It doesn't matter if she was willing or not. She said it wasn't possible. She'd been siphoning money off from the business for a decade. She couldn't pay it back if she tried." He frowned, distracted by a thought. "That's what she said, anyway."

"You don't believe her?"

Erik glanced up at me. His earlier suspicion

returned. "Look, no offense, but I don't know you. I've already told you more than I should have."

I reached into my wallet and withdrew one of the few business cards I carried. He watched me as I put it on the tabletop and slid it toward him. When he didn't reach for it, I pulled out an identification card and showed it to him. The ID had my photo with the word investigator emblazoned across it. It wasn't official, just something I had made up when I decided that showing people my driver's license — complete with my home address — wasn't a great idea.

"Yeah, so?" Erik said, unimpressed.

"Do you want to call Mr. Harrity's office?" I asked. "Or Missy?"

He considered, then waved a hand. "No. I suppose it doesn't matter. I told most of this to the cops anyway."

I put my ID card away. "Do you have a picture of Laura?" I asked him.

"Sure, lots." He motioned toward the wall nearest him.

A number of framed photos hung there. I stepped closer and examined them. The pictures ranged from wedding photos to Erik, Laura, and another couple dressed in Western garb, to action shots of Erik playing hockey and glamor shots of Laura. It was clear the photos covered a considerable amount of time — both Erik and Laura looked much younger in several of them.

"Which one looks most like her today?" I asked

him.

Erik considered, his eyes darting over the collection. Then he pointed to a five-by-seven of Laura. In it, she was coming through the doorway from the kitchen, looking as if she was in a hurry, and dressed in a fancy dress that screamed *bridesmaid*. The shot seemed to have caught her by surprise. Even so, her smile beamed out at the camera.

Warmth radiated from that smile. There seemed to be a special quality to it, a vivacious spark, the kind that made a person want to be around its holder.

Laura Shelton was pretty in a way I thought of as approachable. Her figure was on the thicker side. Dark hair hung just past her shoulders, framing an oval face.

"Looks like she's dressed for a wedding," I said, my eyes locked on Laura's shining smile.

"She was," Erik said. "Maid of honor, in fact."

"Whose wedding?"

"Her sister's."

"Missy's married?" I glanced up in mild surprise. If she had a husband, she hadn't mentioned it.

"No." Erik shook his head. "She was supposed to marry this dude named Chad, but he ghosted her the day of the wedding. Totally split. Left town and everything."

"Why?"

He shrugged. "No clue. Dude was a flake,

though."

"When was this?"

Erik thought about it for a few seconds. "Three years ago, maybe?"

"That's the most recent picture you have of Laura?"

His eyes narrowed. "What's that supposed to mean?"

"Nothing. It's just a question."

He watched me with suspicion briefly. Then he reached into his back pocket and removed his phone. He pecked and swiped at the large square device, then turned the screen toward me. A photo of Laura, seated on the same couch I'd passed on the way to where we now stood, stared out at me. It was an informal casual shot. While her features appeared similar to the one in the bridesmaid dress, there was a different quality to her expression. She looked older. More tired. The smile seemed resigned instead of brilliant. She looked as if life had thoroughly kicked the crap out of her.

"I took this the day before she left," Erik said. His voice had a defensive tone to it.

"Okay," I replied. "I'd like to borrow a photo. In case I need to show it to someone."

Erik considered, then shrugged. "I can text it to you."

I held up my flip phone. "I'm a little behind the times. But go ahead and send it to me."

"What's your number?"

I rattled it off. Erik's fingers danced expertly. A

moment later, my phone buzzed. I ignored it and motioned toward the photograph on the wall. "I'd like to have this one to show to people, too, if that's okay. I'll bring it back when I'm done."

Erik didn't hesitate. He took the frame from the wall and set about removing the photo.

While he worked, I prompted, "You were saying something before about her not being able to pay back the money?"

"It's probably bullshit." He lifted away the photograph backing and handed me the five-by-seven of Laura. I thanked him. He nodded absently and continued. "Anyway, when I suggested she pay back the money, that maybe the old man wouldn't have her arrested if she did, she brushed me off. Personally, I think she has a good chunk of change squirreled away. Maybe she spent some of it, but you can't hide that kind of money. I mean, look at where we live." He motioned to the house around us. "Nothing fancy, I know, but it ain't like I want to lose it."

"How much did she take exactly?" I asked him. "Do you know?"

"Know?" He shook head. "Pines and the cops aren't saying. But I figure it's got to be close to half a mil."

I blinked in surprise. That was significantly more than I expected.

Erik noticed my reaction. "See what I mean? Hard to hide spending that kind of money, so she must have socked it away in a hidey-hole somewhere."

He was probably right. If that number was accurate, a good portion of it was likely in a bank account of some kind. Or in a very big suitcase or duffel bag if it were cash.

"You said you went to your hockey game on Friday night. Was she here when you got back?"

"No."

"What time did you get home?"

"Pretty late," he admitted. "We had a few beers in the locker room after, then me and a couple of the boys hit the bar for a couple more. So… around midnight or one? Maybe later."

"Was her suitcase gone?"

"No," he said. "That's what's weird. I guess she just decided, fuck it. A whole new start. It's not like she couldn't afford it."

"Do you know where she went?"

"No idea."

"If you had to guess?"

He turned up his hands, his eyes turning hard. "Fiji? Shit, man, I don't know. All I know is she bailed on me. Left me high and dry with a giant mess and none of the money. I'll be lucky if I can avoid going bankrupt behind all this."

5

Erik was cooperative enough to share the roster of his recreational hockey team, though he made a point that he didn't see how it would help.

"I don't know that it will," I said. "But you never know for sure what will become important. I like to have options."

That seemed to convince him and he gave me the list of names and numbers.

"I hope you have more luck finding her than the cops have," he said at the door.

"What have they done so far?"

"Not jack shit, you want the truth. Last time I talked to the detective, she seemed more interested in asking questions about me than trying to locate Laura." He flexed his jaw then reached up to scratch the stubble there. "I don't know why I expected more. Whenever we've had a car stolen off the lot, all they do is show up and write down what happened. A clerk could do that."

I paused, still not entirely sure what to make of Erik Shelton. He'd struck me as a bit of a stereotypical used car salesman with his easy good

27

looks and bro-dude mannerisms. Since he wasn't Harrity's client, I didn't owe him anything. Nonetheless, the glaring blind spot he seemed to possess evoked the slightest bit of sympathy in me.

"Do you think," I asked carefully, "there's a chance Laura didn't run off?"

He squinted at me. "Are you dense or something? She's not here." He tapped his chest, miming the same action from earlier in our discussion. "I'm the one dealing with all the shit. Worrying about where she went, when the old man is going to sue, maybe drag my name through the mud and mess up my job in the process…"

I'd stared at him while he ranted, waiting for him to work it out. As he trailed off, it was clear he got my meaning.

Erik frowned. "No," he said emphatically. "I won't believe something bad happened to her. I'm super fucking pissed at her right now, sure. She lied to me and left me holding the bag, but…" He leaned forward, his eyes narrowing further. "Wait. Do you think *I* did something to her?"

"I didn't say that." I kept my words as neutral as possible, even though, if Laura was dead, he remained my number one suspect.

Erik eyed me, his own suspicion returning. "That's what it sounds like to me. It's what that detective was getting at with her questions, too."

"I'm not getting at anything," I said, "other than pointing out one possibility."

"That someone killed her?" Erik snapped.

"That's what you're saying?"

"When someone goes missing—"

"Do you know something you're not telling me?" Erik interrupted, his tone demanding.

"No," I said. "I'm only talking possibilities here."

"Well, that's a shit possibility," he snapped. He waved his hands, irritated. "All this aside, Laura's a good person. No one would want to hurt her."

Not many good people steal six figures from her employer and disappear with it, I thought, but I didn't say it. Instead, I asked Erik to call me if he thought of anything else that might be helpful or if he heard anything about Laura, and I left.

The office for Fresh Pines Cleaning was located in Hillyard, along the neighborhood's core business district on Market Street. The small storefront was flanked on one side by an antique store that doubled as a pawn shop and a barber shop on the other side. A red-haired man in his forties and wearing a white smock stood out front near the curb, smoking.

I tried the door to Fresh Pines but it was locked. I peered inside and saw no one.

"Lunch," the smoking man called to me.

I turned toward him, glancing at my watch. It was ten-thirty. "A bit early," I said.

He shrugged. "Lunch comes early when you start at four-thirty." He shifted his cigarette to his left hand and extended his right. "I'm Ted."

I shook his hand, lifting my chin toward the next-door business. The barber pole rotated in the window, next to the sign that read Hillyard Barber Shop. "That's your shop?"

"Twelve years now."

"That's quite a run."

Ted drew in smoke, watching me. "That's the thing about hair," he said. "Cut it and it always grows back. It's a repeat business."

I glanced up and down the block, not seeing any chain salons. I wasn't surprised. Those larger stores tended to be located at prime locations. Customers would need to go out of their way to come to Ted's.

"What are you looking for?"

"Supercuts," I admitted. "Or the like."

He shook his head. "You won't find their like here. The business association won't allow it. Small, local businesses only."

"That probably helps."

"What helps is being a neighborhood institution. And knowing how to cut hair, of course."

I motioned toward Fresh Pines. "Do you know your neighbors?"

"Sure. They're good people."

"Good people who start way too early in the day," I joked.

Ted smiled slightly. "Can't argue that. But the business dictates the hours, not the other way around. Besides, they don't actually open the front door until eight. All the early morning work goes through the back."

"You seem to know what goes on around here," I said.

"It's my neighborhood."

"You ever talk to anyone who works there?"

Ted took another drag of his cigarette, then lifted a foot and crushed it against the sole of his shoe. "What are you, a bill collector or a process server?"

"Neither. I'm an investigator."

His gaze flicked up and down the length of me. "Not a cop."

"Not anymore. I work for a private attorney."

"Someone suing the old man?"

I shook my head. "Do you know him?"

"Just to say hi to, is all. Him and his daughter run the place."

"What about Laura?"

His eyes widened slightly. "What about her?"

"Do you know her?"

Ted slid his cigarette butt into his pocket and glanced inside his shop. Then he looked back at me. "You ask a lot of questions, buddy, but you don't explain much. Makes me worry that saying anything to you might not be good for the people you're asking about."

"I'm not looking to hurt anyone."

"See, that's what someone aiming to do just that might say." His gaze shifted back to the inside of his shop again. "I gotta go wash my hands and touch up Ernie's flat top."

"I appreciate you talking with me."

Ted eyed me for another moment, as if trying to

decide if I was being sincere. Then he said, "Like I told you, the old man's a good neighbor. Laura's a sweet person. So don't make me regret telling you anything."

In reality, he hadn't told me a damn thing. A few years ago, I'd have told him so. But over the course of working for Harrity, I'd learned better how to talk to people. As a cop, I could often compel them. A uniform and a badge are powerful suggestions and some people saw answering a police officer's questions as a civic duty. As a private citizen, any time someone spoke to me, it was a gift.

So, I did what any decent person might do when receiving a gift.

"Thank you, Ted," I said, and offered my hand again.

Ted paused then shook my hand before heading back into his barber shop. A bell above the door trilled as he entered.

I turned back to the Fresh Pines office, glanced at my watch again, and decided to wait for a while.

6

It turned out that *a while* meant less than fifteen minutes.

While I waited, my phone buzzed. A text from Kylie read Det. Fergus Dow is case investigator.

I texted my thanks and went back to waiting.

Eventually, a wiry man in his early sixties came around the corner of the building, trailed by a woman in her late thirties. He walked in the straight-backed manner I always associated with former military and state patrol troopers. His clothing was casual and neat; a pair of blue slacks and a lighter blue collared shirt, no tie.

The woman was also slender and appeared fit. Even at this distance, it was obvious she spent time in the gym. Her dark brown hair was pulled back in a short ponytail. She wore the same blue shirt, though her loose-fitting slacks were tan.

The man eyed me curiously when he reached the front door. "You looking for work?" he asked me. His gravelly voice sounded like he was already in job interview mode.

"No. I was actually hoping to talk with Lawrence

Pines."

"What about?"

"Are you Lawrence?" I asked.

"No one calls me that," he said. "It's either Larry or Mr. Pines, depending on who you are."

"I'm Stefan Kopriva," I told him. "I've been hired to find Laura Shelton."

His gaze narrowed. Behind him, the woman's nostrils flared and she muttered something I didn't catch. Pines pulled his keys from his pocket and unlocked the front door.

"You can call me Mr. Pines," he said. "You might as well come in."

There was a buzz as the door swung open, announcing our arrival. Inside, he flipped the sign back to OPEN, and made his way through a tiny lobby. "This is my daughter, Serena," he said, and continued through the lobby without looking back.

I held out my hand to her.

She took it, distaste obvious on her face. "It's just Rena," she said. She looked me up and down, seeming unimpressed with me. Then she motioned with her head. "Come on. He'll be headed to the office."

Once we left the entrance area, the majority of the building was full of cleaning equipment and boxes of supplies. The strong scent of industrial cleaners filled my nostrils. Several floor buffers, mops, buckets, and wide brooms lined one wall. No one else was present.

Rena led me toward the office, though I didn't

need her guidance. It was the only open door with a light on. Inside, Pines was already seated behind a utilitarian metal desk, checking over some paperwork. A roughhewn wooden cross as long as my forearm hung directly behind him. Other than that, the walls were bare.

Pines put down the stack of papers and gestured toward the chair across from him. Meanwhile, Rena leaned against the wall off to the side of the desk.

"Who hired you to find Laura?" Pines asked as I sat down. "Was it her husband?"

"Client confidentiality being what it is," I said, "I can't answer that."

He frowned. "Don't I have a right to know? I'm the victim here."

"I'm not the police. But I think your interests are aligned with my client's."

"Because we both want to find Laura and my money?"

I nodded. "The reasons might differ but you both want the same outcome."

He stared at me for a few moments, considering. Then he shrugged and waved his hand. "That sounds reasonable. Go ahead — ask away."

"How long did Laura work for you?"

Pines tilted his head back and looked to the ceiling. "I think I'd only been in business about fifteen months when I hired her. So, seventeen years, she's been with me."

"She kept the books?"

Pines nodded. "She did it all. Invoices, accounts

payable, and payroll. I made the purchasing decisions on anything that wasn't routine, but she handled the paperwork and moved the money."

"You showed a lot of trust," I observed.

Rena snorted. "Yeah, and she stabbed him in the back for it."

Pines raised his hand, not looking Rena's way. She frowned but stopped speaking. "You'll have to forgive my daughter. She's protective of me."

"Understandable," I said. "How big is your business?"

"Why's that matter?"

"I'm just trying to get the lay of the land, is all."

Pines pursed his lips. "We have eighteen employees," he said. "We service twenty-two different clients. Some big, some small."

"I guess what I'm trying to figure out is how much money is flowing through this place every month," I said.

Pines didn't answer. After a few seconds, he leaned forward. "It occurs to me I didn't ask you for any identification," he said.

"No problem." I removed my investigator ID card and handed it to him.

Pines studied it for a moment, then shrugged. "Anyone could get one of these."

Reluctantly, I fished out my state driver's license and showed it to him. He glanced between the two documents before handing the ID card back to me. "All right, you are who you say you are. But you won't say who you're working for, so I—"

"Technically, I work for Joel Harrity," I said. "He's who the client sought out for help."

"The defense attorney?" Pines asked. His expression shifted to something less guarded. "I sent a couple of my guys to him when they ran into trouble a few years ago."

"That was smart." I put my identification cards in my wallet and slipped it back into my pocket. "He's the best in town."

Pines grunted but it didn't sound like disagreement. He watched me for a few more seconds. Finally, he said, "I'm not comfortable sharing my financials with anyone. Not even the cops. The detective asked me to get a forensic audit so they can prosecute Laura when they find her." He shrugged. "If it was only for that purpose, I don't know that I'd pay for it, frankly. Revenge isn't a profitable venture. But my insurance company is insisting on one, too, so I've asked for a few bids from several different firms. In the meantime, I asked Rena to see what she could do."

I glanced over at Rena, whose hard expression hadn't waned. She made me wait before saying, "Near as I can tell, that bitch stole around $250,000."

I let out a low whistle. "Over how long?"

"It started about fifteen years ago."

"Do you know how she did it?"

Rena's lip curled. "How *didn't* she do it? The goddamn bitch took money wherever she could."

"Rena," Pines said, his tone quiet and stern. He gave a short shake of his head. "Don't blaspheme."

Rena rolled her eyes. "Fine." She turned her attention back to me. "Then the *fucking* bitch doctored the records and the monthly reports to cover it up. I had to go back and pull the actual physical paperwork to compare and find where she stole from us."

"Do you have any idea why she did it?"

"Why do thieves steal?" Rena stared at me in disbelief. "Is that really a question?"

"Point taken. How about this—did the amount she embezzled put you at risk for bankruptcy?"

"No," said Rena. "But our insurance policy is general, not specifically crime insurance. They're already making noise about whether this is covered or not. More importantly, Dad wanted to retire this year. Our gross hasn't been high enough these last few years, so he still isn't able to yet. If that $250,000 had gone into an IRA instead of that bitch's purse, it would've made the difference. He'd be able to call it quits and enjoy himself. After working so hard all his life, he deserves it."

I glanced over at Pines. His face had the same hard lines as his daughter but his expression wasn't quite as angry. He saw me looking and gave me a shrug. "It's a significant hit," he admitted. "I'll still get there. Or perhaps I was meant to work straight through to the end."

"Don't say that, Dad," Rena growled. "Don't try to make it easier on her. You gave her a job and trusted her, and she showed her appreciation by stealing from you. For *years*."

"I know," said Pines.

Rena jabbed a finger in my direction. "You or the cops or whoever better find her and get that money back."

"I've been hired to find her," I reminded Rena. "The money is another matter."

She shook her head in disdain. "I should have figured as much. Well, don't worry, we'll sue her ass. Take her shitty house and—"

"Rena," Pines said, this time more softly.

She stopped abruptly, crossing her arms and staring down at the floor, glowering.

"I'm angry, too," Pines said. "If Rena's estimate is accurate, then Laura stole several times our annual profit from me. That's years of my life. I have fewer and fewer of those years left." He took a deep breath and let it out. "There's a part of me, though, that is more heartbroken than angry. I thought of Laura as almost a second daughter to me. It's a betrayal that cuts deep."

"I imagine so," I said.

"Are you a religious man, Mr. Kopriva?"

"No," I answered honestly.

Pines pressed his lips together briefly, as if in disappointment. Then he said, "On the one hand, our Lord preaches forgiveness. I'd like to think, if Laura came to me and confessed her sin, I'd have found a way to forgive her."

Rena scoffed but said nothing.

Pines glanced at her anyway. "Not let the money go, of course. But forgive her, *here*."

He touched his chest, at his heart. Strangely, the action reminded me of Erik Shelton tapping his chest earlier.

"On the other hand," Pines continued, "the Bible teaches us that penance is necessary."

"Penance? What does that mean, exactly?"

Pines leaned forward, his gaze hardening. "It means I want my money back," he growled.

"Finding her is the first step. Do you have any guesses as to where she might be?"

"No clue." Pines spread his hands. "Vegas, maybe?"

"Or hell, I hope," added Rena, her tone remaining harsh. She met my gaze unapologetically. "When I think of Laura sitting on a beach somewhere, sipping goddamn margaritas while Dad has to work another four or five years, it really pisses me off."

Pines gave Rena a look of reproval but didn't correct her for cursing this time. "It makes me angry, too," he admitted. "It also makes me sad."

"Because of the betrayal?" I asked.

He nodded. "It only proves something I've figured out over the long years of my life, even though I wish it weren't true."

"What's that?"

He glanced up at me, his eyes rimmed with resignation. "Only God is constant," he said. "People always disappoint."

7

After interviewing Lawrence Pines and his daughter, Rena, I stopped off at my house to eat some lunch and make a call.

It was a call I never enjoyed making — to the police. Laura's disappearance and/or embezzlement was assigned to River City Police Detective Fergus Dow. That meant hoping for some collaboration if I wanted to get easy access to information.

I pulled up Kylie's text and copied Dow's number into the thin file she'd provided me earlier, then I dialed. The line rang five times and went to voicemail. I was surprised to hear a woman's voice come on and identify herself as Detective Dow. With a name like Fergus, I'd expected a man.

I waited for her standard spiel to end, then left a brief message at the tone. Whether or not she'd call back was anyone's guess, but I decided to give her a while before moving on to the next step in my investigation. This was convenient, since I wasn't exactly certain what that step would be. Another interview with Missy Jardin, probably, and I wasn't looking forward to that.

As I passed my front window, I glanced across the street. A.M. Cannon Park was emblematic of the area of town where I lived. Technically, the neighborhood was called West Central, though a good chunk of it was termed Felony Flats by most River City natives. Cops referred to it as The Zone, a moniker my girlfriend, Anna, confirmed was still in use.

My house was on the fringe of what would be considered The Zone, with Pettit Drive marking the tenuous boundary and A.M. Cannon Park representing a sort of no man's land. As a result, the people who used the park were about as varied as you could get — parents with their young kids, lovers, picnickers, recreational sports enthusiasts, people with dogs (not all of whom cleaned up after their pets), rowdy teenagers, and senior citizens.

It was one of the latter who caught my eye. He sat at a bench that had a concrete table in front of it. A checkerboard was laid out in front of him but his nose was buried in a book. I hadn't noticed him before and the board intrigued me, so I grabbed my cell phone and walked across the street. I approached him and stood nearby, close enough to see he was reading a Tom Clancy novel, and waited for him to notice me. He must have read most of a page before he stabbed a thin finger at his place in the text and looked up at me.

"You gonna say something or stand there like an idjit?" His voice had the slightest trace of an accent, too slight to even place.

"I'm good at the idjit part," I said. "I might just stick with that."

The corner of his mouth twitched in what might have been a smile. He slid an empty matchbook into his paperback and set it on the bench beside him. Then he motioned to the board.

"Do you play?"

"Play?" I asked. "Doesn't everyone? It's checkers, not chess."

He scowled. "Spoken like a true idjit."

I glanced around the park. A few parents watched over kids of various ages while the youngsters climbed on the play structures. A pair of young lovers sat on a blanket, sunning themselves and holding hands. Further away, a group of teenagers smoked and shouted obscenities at each other. No dogs, though, and no frisbee or football players. Except for the teenagers, it was quiet.

"No takers?" I asked him.

He shook his head. "Bunch of cowards."

"You think they're scared of checkers?"

"Nope. Scared of me, though."

I looked him over again and had to agree. The only people in the park that day who might consider approaching him were the loud teenagers, and then only on a dare.

"You should wear a sweater," I suggested. "Like Mr. Rogers. Cultivate that harmless old man look."

"Who are you calling old?" he asked, sizing me up. "You're more mutton than lamb yourself."

I laughed. True enough. "My name's Stef," I said, extending my hand.

He took it. His skin was dry and rough. He squeezed firmly and pumped my hand once. "Mick Darabont," he said.

I motioned to the seat opposite him. Mick nodded his permission. I sat down and studied the board. "Who goes first?" I asked. "I know it's white in chess, but…"

"Black moves first," Mick said.

The black pieces were on his side of the board.

"All right," I said. "I haven't played since I was a kid, but let's do it."

Mick sniffed and moved a piece.

We spent the next fifteen minutes shuffling pieces around the board. It took falling into a couple of stupid traps and getting double-jumped before the flow of the game came back to me. By that time, I was fighting a losing battle and the only real goal became prolonging my own defeat.

Finally, Mick maneuvered my last remaining checker into a corner. Regardless of which space I moved, he was poised to jump my piece and win.

I turned over my hands. "Checkmate," I said.

He scowled. "This is checkers," he said, his voice raspy. "It isn't chess. You don't get to surrender. You win or you lose." He dipped his chin toward the board. "Now, move your man."

I slid the checker diagonally to the left.

Mick grinned and jumped it with his king. Triumphantly, he collected my piece and added it to the stack next to the board.

"Good game," I said, not really meaning it.

"You played like a child," Mick said, matter-of-factly. "At least, at first. Then you fought like a man."

"Go again?" I asked.

Mick nodded slowly. "Sure."

As we re-ordered the pieces, my phone buzzed. Mick frowned as I answered it. "Hello?"

"This is Detective Dow, River City Police. You left me a message earlier."

"I did. Thanks for calling me back."

While we spoke, Mick swiftly put the last of the pieces back into their starting positions.

"I'm on my way to an interview," Dow said, "but I can work you in if you can meet me in the next twenty minutes."

"I can do that. At the station, or…?"

"I'm in my car. How about the parking lot of the car wash at Boone and Ash?"

"I'll be there," I told her.

She hung up without another word.

I stood. "Sorry," I told Mick. "Duty calls. Another time?"

"Sure," he said, his tone dismissive. He reached for his novel, not bothering to look at me. "Another time."

8

Detective Fergus Dow was already at the car wash when I arrived. Her unmarked police vehicle, one of the newer Impalas, was backed into the corner of the parking lot well away from other vehicles. I drove toward her, instinctively knowing her intent. When I pulled to a stop next to her car, our driver's side windows were directly across from each other.

It was a common police tactic for meeting while on patrol. Some called it car-siding, others said it was a roadside, but it meant the same. I wondered if Dow knew about my background or if she'd simply parked this way out of habit.

Dow was talking on her phone with the window raised. She made brief eye contact with me and held up a finger. Then she looked away and continued her conversation.

I slid down my window and waited.

About a minute later, she disconnected and rolled down her window. When our eyes met, I sensed the coldness there. That made me think she knew who I was, something that wasn't as common as it used to be among RCPD members. When you make a mistake as devastating as the one I made, people tend to remember.

"Let's be clear," Dow said. "I'm here because I have a soft spot for Mr. Pines. He's a nice old man. He didn't deserve what happened to him."

"Understood." For a long time, I told myself I didn't care why a cop was helping me, as long as I got the help. It's not like it happened often anyway. In reality, though, I knew I *did* care, so a more accurate way to put it was I'd learned to deal with it. "Either way, thank you."

She didn't acknowledge my thanks. Instead, she said, "What do you want to know?"

"How are you treating this case?" I asked.

Her eyes narrowed with suspicion. "Same as I handle every case. No special treatment."

"I mean, is it a missing person? A fraud?"

"Both," Dow said. "Laura Shelton appears to have embezzled money from her employer. Once confronted, she subsequently disappeared."

"You think she's on the run?"

"Have you ever heard of Occam's razor?" Dow asked. "Simplest answer is usually the correct one?"

"Of course."

"Well, there's your answer. The most likely scenario is she fled to avoid prosecution."

I couldn't argue so I asked, "If you find her, do you have enough PC to charge her?"

Dow brow scrunched in thought. Then she said, "Probable cause is a fluid concept. I think there's enough. My sergeant or the prosecutor might have a different opinion." Her lip curled. "Your employer definitely will."

"Probably," I agreed, "but that's his job."

Dow sniffed and said nothing.

"Fraud investigations usually go to the General Detectives, right?"

She nodded stiffly.

"But a missing persons case is Major Crimes," I observed.

"Your point being…?"

"Your voicemail said you were in the G.D., so I'm just trying to get a handle on how the department views this case. If you saw it as an actual missing person, wouldn't it go to Major Crimes labeled as the same? The fraud element would be more of a kicker than the primary designator."

Dow regarded me for a few moments. When she spoke, her tone was cold and biting. "Look, I know who you are. I know what you did when you were on the job, and I know the shit you've been up to since. None of it affects me, so I figure live and let live. My focus is on serving the victim, which is Mr. Pines in this situation. But do me a favor and don't pretend like you know anything about how our department works."

I held up my hands. "No offense meant. I did work there for four years."

"Just long enough to fuck up real good," Dow said, her voice still icy.

Anger brewed in my gut, but I kept it from boiling. More than fifteen years had passed since I made the fatal error that cost Amy Dugger her life. The shame still burned. So did the grief. But I'd learned over the last few years to control the anger that also came with it. The shame and grief ate at my soul, but the anger got me in the most trouble.

"All right," I said, my jaw tight. "How about you explain it to me, then?"

Dow's calculating gaze never left my face. "The case was classified as a missing person. It went to Major Crimes, but their caseload was heavy, so it spilled over to my unit. That's how I got the case."

I nodded slowly. "Where are you with it?" I asked.

"Officially? It's suspended."

I raised a brow. "Suspended? Why?"

"Because I've run through all the leads and taken all of the actions I can at this point."

"But she's still missing."

"And I keep getting new cases assigned," Dow said. "When I run out of moves, my supervisor suspends the case."

I mulled that over. I'd expected this to still be an active investigation. "So, you're just done with it? Case closed?"

"I didn't say closed. I said suspended."

"What's that mean, exactly?"

She shrugged. "Think of it as pushing the pause button and filing it away until something unpauses it."

"What would it take to make that happen?"

"The biggest would be finding Laura Shelton.

That would close out the missing person case entirely and I'd move forward with the fraud."

"You've suspended the fraud angle, too, then?"

She nodded. "I've got all the information I can gather at the moment. If Laura shows up, I'll interview her and make a decision on the disposition."

"You'd charge her?"

"If it were up to me, yes."

"Then why not get a warrant for her right now?" I asked. "That way—"

"Two reasons," Dow interrupted. "For one, a missing person locate is still out for her. That's in NCIC, so it's nationwide." She eyed me briefly. "That's a database. The National Crime—"

"I know what NCIC is." I took a calming breath before continuing. "Can you give me a summary of what you did? I don't want to duplicate effort if I don't need to."

The last part was a lie. In all likelihood, I'd tread over every inch of ground I could, even if Detective Dow had already done so. I wanted to push through her hostility, though, so this was the best I could do when it came to offering an olive branch.

I couldn't tell if it worked, but Dow answered my question. "I searched the house. Nothing there and no sign of a struggle. I ran a check on her credit cards and bank activity." She shook her head. "Nothing there, either."

"You talked to her husband?"

"Of course."

"Did you suspect him of being involved?"

Dow pressed her lips together briefly. "I didn't find any evidence of foul play."

"That's the first place you'd look, isn't it? If you thought something happened to Laura?"

She nodded. "Occam's razor, again. But there was no sign of anything. And his alibi checks out with multiple witnesses."

I thought about it. In most cases of murder, the killer was someone close to the victim. Often, it was a spouse. My first thoughts about Erik had been in that direction. True crime shows have made examining such cases a staple of American television over the past several decades. In those instances, there were always telltale signs. Red flags leading up to the murder and suspicious behavior afterward. Those seemed to be missing here, at least for the most part.

"Killing your wife and then going to play hockey seems pretty cold," I mused aloud.

"It is," Dow agreed. "There's also no evidence anything like that happened to Laura Shelton."

I watched her carefully. She was a cold woman, at least outwardly so. But there'd been something in her reaction when I asked about Erik, so I pressed harder.

"Was something off about the husband?" I asked. "Maybe not criminal, but...?"

She blinked but her expression remained otherwise impassive. "Like I said, there was no evidence of foul play."

"You're ruling out the possibility she might have been murdered?"

"I haven't ruled out anything. At the moment, my official stance is she is a missing person."

"Unofficially?"

Dow shifted slightly in her seat. "Unofficially, she probably fled when she expected to be arrested for embezzlement."

"But no charge is pending," I noted.

"Not at the moment."

"Mr. Pines said you asked for a forensic audit?"

She nodded. "The prosecutor requires one if we're going to charge her."

"He said he didn't really want to spend the money."

"That's his prerogative. The case won't go forward without one."

"Maybe that's what he wants," I said. "I got the feeling he was a bit reluctant to see her go to jail."

"There's no question about that," Dow said. She shrugged. "I've seen it before. He's going through the process of reporting the crime and getting the audit for insurance purposes. Most likely, he'll eventually get to the point where he'll want to press charges. Right now, I think most of the momentum for that is coming from the daughter."

"You think he might not follow through?"

"If I had to guess," said Dow, "I think he's hoping to get back at least a portion of what she stole. Especially if his insurance doesn't cover the loss. In some of these cases, victims will forgo charges for partial recovery and a repayment plan. You can't get money very easily out of an inmate."

I digested her words. Most everything she said meshed with what little I'd learned so far.

Dow glanced at her dashboard clock. "I've only a few minutes longer. Anything else?"

"What about the sister, Missy? What do you make of her?"

"No opinion." Dow's voice was flat. "I talked to her. She said she didn't know anything about her sister's whereabouts. Or the embezzlement, for that matter."

"Could she be covering for Laura?"

"Anything's possible." Dow's tone sounded doubtful. "Pretty extravagant play though if that's the case. Her hiring your boss, I mean."

I didn't respond. Instead, I was thinking of a common theme I'd heard from almost everyone. "It's kind of an odd situation, isn't it?"

"Not really," said Dow. "People steal all the time. They run away all the time."

"Laura doesn't seem the type," I said.

Dow raised a brow slightly. "You know her that well already, huh?"

"I'm not saying that, but—"

"She's *exactly* the type," Dow interrupted. "Most embezzlement cases involve smaller businesses, not huge corporations. Most suspects are women in their forties with accounting responsibilities. Typically unmarried so that's different in this case. Otherwise, Laura Shelton fits the profile pretty well."

"I thought you guys weren't supposed to profile anymore," I joked.

Dow's cold stare didn't relent. "Anything else?"

"No," I said. "If something comes up, I'll give you a call."

Dow dropped her car into gear. "I'll lie awake at night with anticipation." She pulled away.

I sat in my Celica for a few moments after she left, replaying the conversation in my mind. Despite Dow's frigid response, the interaction actually went better than I expected. There weren't any revelations but I felt like the picture was slowly filling in. Not enough yet, though.

I reached for my notes, picked up my phone and made a call.

9

Kent Harper was a thick-bodied man, slightly below average height, with a round face. My initial impression of him was he was fat. While he may have been carrying an extra layer, when he shook my hand, his strength was obvious. He moved with athletic grace, as well.

On the phone, the man had been reluctant to share any information with me.

"I don't know who you are," he'd said. "If you're legit, come by the shop and we'll talk."

The shop meant Doc's Muffler Clinic, a muffler repair and installation shop on North Division Street. Harper was working on a car on a lift when I arrived. He directed me to the tiny office nearby while he finished. A few minutes later he came into the office, wiping his hands on a blue rag.

"You have ID?" he asked.

I showed him my investigator identification card. His lip twisted and his expression remained dubious. I withdrew my driver's license and held it out to him with my finger over my address. He peered at that and nodded his approval.

"Just being careful," he told me. "No offense meant."

"None taken."

"What can I do for you?"

"You're the team captain for the hockey team?"

"Team captain and sponsor," Harper said. "Why?"

"I'm trying to find Erik Shelton's wife," I said.

Harper winced slightly. "That's too bad, what happened there. Not a surprise, exactly, but too bad."

"Not a surprise?"

Harper finished wiping his hands and stuffed the rag into a pocket of his dark blue coveralls. "I mean, she was bound to find out about all the running around he was doing, right? Can't keep that shit secret forever. Once it comes out? Divorce City."

A small jolt went through me. "Erik was having an affair?"

"*An* affair?" Harper laughed derisively. "Dude was a straight up hound dog. Chasing trim was all he and his buddies talked about in the locker room."

"His buddies? Are you talking the whole team, or...?"

Harper shook his head. "I brought him and two others on a couple of years ago when I lost several players in the off season. A couple moved away and one had to quit when the baby came. Anyway, they all worked together with Santos, who was already on the team. Santos is a good guy, so I figured they'd be okay, too."

"They weren't?"

Harper shrugged. "Let's put it this way — not my kind of people. I've been married seventeen years to the same woman. I take it seriously. These guys…" He waved a hand in the air. "…they obviously don't."

I recognized the name Santos from the roster Erik had given me. I took it from my file and showed it to Harper. "This is the team, right?"

"Yep. That's the roster I gave every player. Here're his buddies." He pointed to a pair of names and I put tick marks next to them. "I don't know what good it'll do you talking to them. Whatever he asks them to back him up on, they'll do it."

"What makes you say that?"

"Because they did it all the time. Giving each other alibis so their wives and girlfriends didn't catch on to all of the skirt chasing they do." Harper shook his head in disgust. "Look, I'm not a church man or anything, and I say live and let live. But it got to where I had to put the kibosh on talking about women in the locker room, just so I didn't have to hear about their goddamn little adventures. I play hockey for fun, not to be aggravated."

"How long ago did you ban that sort of talk?"

Harper's forehead scrunched in thought. "A couple months ago."

"You knew about Laura?"

"Yes, of course. That's family talk, not poon hound talk. Erik was looking for some sympathy and most of the team gave it to him."

"You didn't?"

Harper twisted his lips before answering. Then he sighed. "If she stole that money like the cops think, that's wrong. I own a small business, so I know how devastating that can be. So, I can't exactly feel too bad for a thief, if she is one."

"And Erik?"

"Like I told you, her getting out of Dodge is something he probably had coming. I don't condone the stealing part, but the leaving Erik part seems like the right move to me."

I slipped the roster back into the thin file and tucked it under my arm. "Doesn't sound like you like Erik very much."

"I wouldn't say that," said Harper. "I don't respect him, though. Him and his work buddies throw off the chemistry of the team. Honestly, I wish I'd never brought them on, even though he's a pretty skilled player. He fills the net on a regular basis, and goals are how we keep score. Aside from that, I'd have been better off taking my chances with random guys from the sign-up pool."

"Santos, too?"

"Naw, he's good people. I get the sense he regrets vouching for them."

"Think he'd talk to me?"

Harper shrugged. "Maybe. Hard to tell for sure where his loyalties lie. He's more likely to tell you the truth than Erik's other buddies."

I slipped the list back into my pocket. "Sounds

like you're dealing with a lot of locker room drama."

"You could say that. When everybody sticks to talking hockey and playing it, things aren't so bad." Harper glanced over my shoulder. "That's my three o'clock pulling in now," he said. "If I don't get him rolling, I'm going to be here past closing again."

I took my cue. "I appreciate your help," I said, offering my hand.

Harper shook it. "No problem. I hope it works out."

"So do I. One last question?"

"Make it quick," said Harper.

"Any idea who Erik was seeing?"

Harper pressed his lips together. "I tried not to listen, so…"

"Anything you can think of might help."

Harper thought about it for a few moments. Then he said, "The only one I can think of was a woman named Hailey. She was a bartender at The Swinging Doors. The only reason I remember is because they were making jokes about the comet."

"That's Halley's," I said.

"I know." Harper gave me a tight grin. "I might change out mufflers for a living, but I'm not as dumb as those guys."

_10_

After I left Doc's Muffler Clinic, I parked in the lot of Franklin Park Mall and made a few calls. Most of Erik's teammates didn't answer. I didn't bother leaving messages for them, though I did leave one for Oliver Santos.

I saved Erik's best pals for last. I considered finding out their addresses and interviewing them in person but, after talking to Harper, I didn't want to give Erik any more time to coach them than he'd already had. After some consideration, I decided to call instead.

Steve Logge answered his phone. He was one of the two Harper had pointed out. He flatly refused to answer any questions, even after I told him Erik gave me his number.

"I need to check with the E-Dog before I talk to you," he said, his tone self-important.

Kevin Warrington was initially helpful, though he sounded disinterested for most of the brief conversation. When I brought up the subject of the three of them fooling around with other women, he threw on the brakes immediately.

60

"Dude, not cool," was all he said, and hung up.

I knew calling them and getting on the topic of skirt-chasing was a risky approach. At the same time, something I've noticed about guys who like the hunt is they are often happy to brag about it if they think you're of a similar mindset. I tried to subtly convey that sentiment to both Logge and Warrington and neither one bought it.

No loss, really, if Harper was right about them probably backing up whatever story Erik wanted to tell.

After I finished with my calls, I leaned back in my seat and closed my eyes. My immediate reaction to learning Laura had discovered Erik was fooling around was to suspect him even more than I had before. My initial suspicion of him was natural but Detective Dow's lukewarm assessment of the situation blunted my concerns. Now, those concerns were back.

A divorce, whether actual or threatened, is a major upheaval in someone's life. The resulting stress has accounted for plenty of instances in which one party or the other reacted radically. That could be the case for either Laura or Erik here. If Laura took off, that was an extreme reaction... at least to the marital strife. It was a bit less extreme if she thought she was looking at prosecution.

For Erik's part, could he have killed Laura rather than divorce her?

I couldn't say. In fact, without more information, I couldn't even guess. What was their relationship like? He had seemed more upset about the fallout of her theft and him getting sued than the fact she was gone. Was that because he believed she was hiding somewhere with the money? Or because he knew *exactly* where she was, because he put her there? If so, his outrage would be a carefully constructed act.

I realized I'd missed asking an important question when I first interviewed Erik. What was their overall financial situation? If their finances were stressed, Erik learning about the embezzlement could make for a volatile argument. Then again, so could his messing around with other women.

My eyes opened a slit, letting in some light. I decided there was only one way to get a better handle on these possibilities. I put the car in gear and left the lot.

Erik Shelton answered the door, still looking disheveled. His eyes narrowed when he saw me. "What do *you* want?"

"To talk," I said.

"Sounds like you've been doing some talking already," he sneered. "Stevie and Kevin both called."

"I told you I'd contact them."

"Yeah, well, you didn't say you were going to talk shit to them."

"I'm only asking questions," I said. I motioned toward the doorway. "Can I come in? I want to talk to you some more."

"About what?"

I didn't answer, waiting him out. After a few seconds, he scowled but opened the door. This time, he didn't lead me deeper into the house, however. He stood on the small landing and stared at me.

"What do you want to know?"

"You said you and Laura were arguing the last night she was here."

"Yeah, so?"

"What was the argument about?"

Erik's scowl deepened. "Didn't we already talk about this?"

"Humor me," I said. "Was it about money or your affairs?"

"I didn't have any affairs."

I frowned. "Erik, I don't care if you did. That's between you and your wife. I only want to find her."

"If you don't care and it's between us, why are you asking?"

"Anything that helps me find her is worth asking about," I said.

Erik considered that, his expression dubious.

"I think she found out," I said. "But my bigger question is if that meant a divorce."

Erik shook his head. "No way, man. We were solid."

"Then what was the argument about?"

Erik glanced away, not answering.

"You *do* want to find her, don't you?" I asked.

"Of course."

"Then help me do that."

"I don't see how talking about this helps."

I ignored his protest. "Were the two of you getting a divorce?"

"No!" he said sharply, his gaze snapping to mine. "I already told you that. Jesus!"

"Then what was the argument about?"

Erik bit his lip. "Look," he said. "Every couple has issues but we were *not* splitting up."

"Okay."

"As for seeing other women on the side…" He trailed off with a shrug. "It's true. I've had a few one-offs. I figured Laura knew about it."

"You're saying she *knew?*"

Erik bobbed his head. "I think so, yeah. I mean, not the details. Just that it happened from time to time. It was part of our…" He shrugged again, "…unspoken agreement, I guess you'd call it. Laura wasn't very interested in sex anymore, all right? For me, it's more of a constant. This was how I handled it."

"What do you mean by *this*, exactly?"

"I took off a piece here and there," Erik said. "Always quiet-like. Never so she had to know about it. It wasn't in her face, so she could pretend. We both could."

I watched him, looking for signs of deception. His slick used-car salesman demeanor made it difficult to discern what was true, what was half-true, and what was flat out lies. Then a thought occurred to me.

"That was what the argument was about," I said. "She found out details?"

Erik turned over his hands. "It was old news, from a couple of years ago."

"If it was old news, why bring it up again now?"

"I don't know. Could've been all the stress about the money she stole. Or, since we were fighting about that, maybe she wanted to turn the blame back onto me. Focus on my supposed crimes."

"Crimes?" I cocked my head at the word.

He frowned. "Not like that. It was about me fooling around. She heard from someone who said we had a thing."

"Heard from who?"

"Who knows?" Erik said. "She wouldn't say."

"Was it true?"

Erik's eyes narrowed. "Why do you care about that?"

"It's like I told you," I said. "I'm pulling every loose string I can. You never know what will lead to finding Laura."

Erik rubbed his chin thoughtfully. "I don't see it. How is talking to women I maybe banged going to help you find my wife?"

"I don't know. That's the point."

He eyed me dubiously. "Look, this isn't some after-hours Cinemax flick. Laura didn't run off with one of my side pieces or something. Our marriage isn't even the issue here. She stole a bunch of money from her work and took off when she got caught, leaving me holding the bag. You're barking up the wrong tree."

"I'd still like to talk to these other women."

"What, are you some kind of pervert?"

"No."

"Then fuck off with that." He pointed toward the door. "Go do what you were hired to do. Find my wife."

I made no move to leave. "I'm trying to," I said. "I need your help."

"I'm not saying another word about our marriage."

"All right," I said. "There's something else."

"What?"

"I'd like to see your bank statements over the past year."

Erik's eyes narrowed further. "The hell?" He reached out and grasped the doorknob, and jerked open the door. He jabbed a finger toward the exit. "Get the fuck out of my house."

11

The Swinging Doors was on Francis Avenue just west of Monroe Street. It had been there for as long as I could remember, making it almost a River City landmark. The place was more of a sports bar than a serious drinking establishment. It didn't surprise me Erik Shelton and his teammates chose it as their post-game destination.

The smell of freshly cooked French fries hung in the air as I entered. I made my way to the bar and took a seat. The majority of the tables were empty and a lone bartender stood watching me. She was in her early fifties and had thin hair pulled back into a limp ponytail. She dressed like she wanted to look thirty; low-cut jeans with a baseball shirt tucked in.

"What can I get for you?" she asked.

I ordered a tonic. Wordlessly, she dumped ice into a glass and filled it. Then she slid a slice of lime onto the lip and plunked it down in front of me.

"Any food today?"

I shook my head, looking around. "Not too busy in here yet."

"It'll get that way soon," she said. "Calm before the storm."

She started to move away, but I stopped her.

"What's your name?" I asked.

"Viola."

"Nice name."

She gave me a tired look. "Thanks. Anything else?"

"Is Hailey working?"

The tired look became a scowl. "Who's asking?"

"My name's Stef."

Viola stepped closer. "Hailey comes in later. What do you want with her?"

"To talk."

"Mmm-hmmm." Viola stopped in front of me. "Listen, Hailey's a nice girl. She's friendly to everyone. If she was friendly to you, it didn't mean anything special except that's how she is."

"It's not like that," I said. "I'm not trying to date her."

"I know what you're trying to do."

I started to object then tilted my head. "Wait. Are you her mother?"

"Aunt," Viola said. "Which means I'm even more likely to eighty-six someone bothering Hailey."

"I don't plan to bother her at all," I said. "Just talk to her for a couple of minutes." I withdrew my investigator card and put it on the bar. "Just some background on a case," I added.

"You're a cop?" she asked.

"No," I said. "I used to be. Now I'm private."

There was a fair amount of deception and almost

as much truth in that statement. Nothing I said was a technical lie. I've discovered people tend to jump to conclusions. Sometimes those conclusions work in my favor. For instance, most people looked at me, took a guess at my age, and took the used to be a cop statement to mean I was retired off the job. A certain amount of credibility and trust came with that assumption, even if it wasn't the truth. Most people also heard me say the word "private" and thought it meant I was a licensed private investigator. That also lent me some credibility and it also wasn't the truth. Most people never realized that. A few, however, didn't necessarily make those assumptions.

Viola seemed like the second sort. Her suspicion didn't waver. She didn't look down at my card right away, keeping her eyes fixed on me as if trying to pry out my true motive. Finally, she glanced down, she said, "That looks fake."

"It's real," I assured her. "So am I. Now, what time does Hailey get in?"

Viola crossed her arms. "She gets in at fuck off o'clock."

"Come on."

Viola reached out and pulled away my tonic. "Whenever she does come in, I'll be sure to tell her you were here and not to talk to you about anything. Meanwhile, you're eighty-sixed." She dumped out the liquid and slapped the glass onto a rubber dish tray. "I don't like sneaks," she said.

I got up and left.

12

People are strange.

Some prefer a direct, straight-to-the-point, no-nonsense conversation. Viola was clearly one of those. Others require some sort of rapport building ahead of talking about sensitive subjects. It's almost like they need to establish some degree of trust before moving forward. People like Viola, however, already know they're not going to trust me, so they just want to get on with it.

Figuring out which is which can be the difference between cooperation and… well, and Viola.

I decided to stop off to see Harrity and update him. I also wanted his advice on something. A quick glance at the time told me I might still catch him at his office.

The area around the courthouse and public safety campus was especially busy, so I had to park two blocks away. I took my time walking down the sidewalk. Since losing the bottom of my left leg below the knee, I've slowly grown used to the prosthetic, but it still gave me a slight hitch in my gait. My physical therapist once told me this was a learned behavior born of my own distrust for the mechanical soundness of the device.

She was probably right.

Nonetheless, I walked at an easy pace everywhere I went, never hurrying unless I had to. I knew this drove Anna crazy because she's a fast walker. She never uttered a word in complaint, though, and adjusted to my walking speed whenever we were together.

The short walk did me good. It gave me an opportunity to sort through what I'd learned so far. From the morass of questions and suspicions, a couple of possible scenarios were forming. Truth be told, they were the same two I started with and now both of them seemed even more probable.

The door to Harrity's office was unlocked, which was a bit of good luck. It was after five and there were days when the lawyer kept banker's hours.

Kylie sat at the receptionist desk. Her computer screen was dark and her purse on the desk in front of her. She gave me a smile tinged with some disappointment.

"He's about five minutes from calling it a day," she told me in a tone that matched her expression.

I understood the reason for the disappointment in her voice. She was ready to leave. My arrival threatened to delay her departure.

"I'll be fast," I assured her, and headed back.

Harrity's office door stood open about a foot, his classic sign he could be bothered if necessary. I knocked on the frame and pushed the door open further, sticking my head in. He glanced up from the paperwork he was reading.

"You got a minute?"

"How many minutes?" he replied easily.

"Ten or so."

"Of course." He put the paperwork down and gestured me inside.

"All right if I kick Kylie loose first?" I asked him.

He spread his hands. "If you don't think we'll need her."

"We won't."

I made the short trip down the hall to Kylie's desk. She was looking at her phone, a newer, larger model more like a small computer compared to the tiny flip phone I carried.

"He says you can take off," I told her.

Kylie's smile was more genuine this time. "Thanks, Stef." She gathered up her purse and headed for the door. I followed her, twisting the lock behind her. Then I returned to Harrity's office.

The lawyer was looking at paperwork again when I entered. He set it aside, folded his hands, and leaned back in his big, leather chair. I sat down across from him and put my notepad on the chair beside me. "This one is messy," I said.

"How so?"

"Where to start?" I said. "It's all problematic."

"Start with the client," Harrity told me.

"All right. She doesn't make sense to me."

"In what way?"

I spread my hands. "Why does she think she needs an attorney? Was she involved in the embezzlement somehow? Or her sister's disappearance?"

"Do you think she's involved in either one?"

"I don't know. It strikes me as odd she ended up in your office in the first place. Not to mention that, somehow, *I need a lawyer* turned into hiring a private investigator."

Harrity didn't react to my words. He merely watched me and waited for me to continue.

So, I said, "I talked to the victim of the embezzlement, Lawrence Pines. He seemed equal parts hurt, disappointed, and angry. Said Laura was like a daughter to him. After my conversation with the investigating detective, I'm fairly convinced that he's a reluctant victim."

"Meaning?"

"Meaning he's probably wishy-washy on pressing charges, especially if he can recover some of the missing money."

"The money isn't missing," Harrity corrected. "It was stolen. Laura Shelton is missing, however."

"I'm getting to that," I said. "Let's stick with Mr. Pines for a second. He's still taking bids on getting a forensic audit, so an accurate accounting of what was stolen isn't in the cards anytime soon. Meanwhile, all we've got is his daughter's estimate."

"Do you have any reason to doubt her figures?"

"No," I admitted. "I'd imagine she's accurate. In

the ballpark, anyway. Then again, she seemed angry enough at Laura to inflate those numbers, so you never know."

"Does it matter?" Harrity asked. "If the father declines to press charges, then I suspect their most pressing concern will be civil recovery."

"I suppose." I shrugged. "It just strikes me odd that someone would get a quarter of a million dollars stolen and not want to see the embezzler who did it go to jail."

"You're looking at it through the lens of justice," Harrity said. "A businessman looks at it through a different lens. Even so, people's responses are unpredictable."

I almost smiled at that, hearkening back to my earlier thought. "They can be strange," I agreed. "Which brings me to the husband, Erik."

"You suspect his involvement?"

"In the embezzlement? No." I gave Harrity a meaningful look. "Look, everyone is assuming Laura ran away with all that money. Maybe she did. But what if her husband killed her?"

Harrity pursed his lips. I knew he'd seen plenty in his career; far too much to dismiss this scenario out of hand, even if it did sound like some true crime TV show exposé.

"Did the police investigate this possibility?"

"They did."

"And?"

"The detective said there was no evidence to support the idea."

"But you remain dubious," Harrity observed.

"You pay me to be skeptical," I said. "Erik Shelton doesn't act like someone whose wife committed a crime and fled."

"How does one act in that situation?"

"Not as unconcerned about her as he did when I talked to him," I told Harrity. "He was far more concerned about getting sued by Pines than where she might be. Not to mention, he's a cheater."

Harrity arched a brow. "He's having an affair?"

"Multiple ones, it seems. They were fighting about it."

Harrity considered the news for a few moments. Then he motioned for me to continue.

"I mentioned the police before," I said, "so I'll finish up with that part of the puzzle. Not only has the detective seemingly discounted the potential for Erik having harmed Laura, but her supervisor suspended the case."

Harrity tilted his head. "Then they have ceased looking for Laura Shelton?"

I nodded. "Actively, at least. There's a missing person report on her. That's nationwide, so if she's stupid enough *not* to assume a new identity *and* if a cop comes across her for some reason, RCPD will get a call. I assume that would re-open the case and they'd proceed with the embezzlement investigation. That might not happen if Mr. Pines doesn't ultimately cooperate to the level they need him to in order to prosecute."

"In essence, then," Harrity said, "active police

involvement in this matter has largely ceased."

"Pending further developments, exactly."

"That is unfortunate for our client but not a wholly negative development."

"Because the cops won't feel like I'm stepping on their toes if the case is suspended?"

"Precisely."

I didn't argue. He was mostly correct. Though, where I was concerned, I was relatively sure they'd be able to work up some agitation regardless.

"Is there any more?" Harrity asked.

"Not really. I wanted to bring you up to speed, and get your take on what I'm seeing."

"My take?" Harrity mused. "Very well, here are my thoughts in the same order you presented them to me."

I waved for him to proceed.

"First, the client," Harrity began. "It is my assessment she has a malleable personality. Her friend—"

"Dania," I said. I lifted my notepad. "I still need to talk to her, too."

"I believe Dania's concerns for Missy were mercenary in nature. Perhaps she believed Missy had some sort of financial stake in the outcome of this situation, which is ignorant on her part. However, due to her impressionable nature, Missy acquiesced. In all likelihood, this was also driven by her concern for her sister's safety."

"So, you trust her?"

"Trust is irrelevant. Her motivation seems

natural and genuine — to find Laura."

"All right," I conceded, though I was unconvinced.

"Continuing with Mr. Pines," Harrity said. "His response does not seem out of the ordinary, especially for a family-owned business. Laura was a long-time employee. You said he thought of her as a daughter. Hesitance to prosecute is not surprising. Nor is his own daughter's anger."

I shrugged. "True enough."

"Do you have any reason to suspect Mr. Pines?" Harrity asked.

I considered. "As in, he found out about the money and killed Laura?"

Harrity dipped his chin ever so slightly in response. "If so, he wouldn't want anyone looking into the missing money because it might expose his own culpability."

"Or any other shady business he might be up to," I added, thinking it through. Finally, I gave Harrity a dubious expression. "I doubt it. He doesn't seem the type. The only object hanging on his office wall was a foot-long cross. He brought up God more than once in our short conversation."

"A religious exterior can conceal any number of evils," Harrity said.

"No argument. It's possible, but I don't think so."

"All right," Harrity continued. "I'll trust your assessment. Turning to the husband now. While infidelity certainly presents as motive in many cases, if the police have discovered no reason to suspect him, I would tend to accept that judgment. At least until further evidence is presented."

I raised my eyebrows. "Way to eviscerate my concerns."

"Just applying logic."

"I use logic," I said.

"You do," said Harrity. "However, you also rely on intuition. Intuition is an excellent tool to further an investigation but it has no place when it comes to formulating a conclusion."

"So me thinking something's off about Erik…?"

"Means perhaps you should investigate further. Nothing more."

"All right."

"Lastly, the police." Harrity drew in a deep breath and steepled his fingers. "We both know from a long history of interaction with RCPD, in particular, that in most instances, we cannot influence the course of action the police intend to take. We also know the level of cooperation borders between grudging at best and the absolute legal minimum at worst. Thus, I suspect you will have to consider any help from that arena as a bonus."

"I kinda figured that."

"What is your intended course of action?" Harrity asked.

"I'd like to see Laura's financial records."

"The husband is the most likely source of those."

"He is," I agreed. "But *fuck off* seemed like a no to me."

Harrity frowned at my use of profanity but didn't address it directly. Instead, he said, "The police likely have those records."

"I think you're right. I also think, if I did a public records request, they'd be completely redacted for privacy reasons."

"Possibly." The slightest trace of an ironic smile appeared on Harrity's lips. "It would seem you might need to ask the detective for a favor, after all."

"Yay," I said, unenthusiastically.

"What's your purpose in examining the records?"

"My primary purpose is what you asked me to do—find Laura. Her personal finances might shed some light in a way that will help me do that." I shrugged. "So might the business records."

"That may be the place to start," Harrity suggested. "Perhaps Mr. Pines will be more willing to help than Detective Dow."

"Maybe," I said doubtfully. "The main fact still remains—I don't know if Laura Shelton is on the run, hiding somewhere, or dead."

"Is that the order of probability?" Harrity asked. "In your estimation?"

I considered. On the run? She'd been missing for a week-and-a-half. If she was running *to* someplace, I imagined she'd made it there by now. If so, she wasn't running any longer; she was hiding out. Was that more likely than someone having killed her?

I thought about Erik for a few long seconds. Did he have it in him to kill his wife? Over what? His dalliances? According to him, she already knew. Could he be lying about that?

Of course, he could. He could also be lying about a potential reason for killing Laura — all the heat over the stolen money. He was potentially facing financial ruin. Then again, maybe he believed she had the money and he killed her trying to get it. Or any other reason that existed in human perfidy. People commit murder all the time, and for motives that seem foreign to most of us.

Did Erik have it in *him* to do so? That was the question.

"I don't know enough to handicap this one," I told Harrity. "Most likely, she ran off with the money and is hiding somewhere, trying to figure out what comes next. There's a non-zero chance someone killed her, too. If that happened, Erik is my number one suspect at the moment."

"What of Mr. Pines or his daughter?"

"Lower on the list," I said. "There're too many unknowns. For all I know, it could have been someone else or something completely random. Or, like I said, she's holed up in a motel, trying to figure out the best place to hide permanently."

"Still much to explore," Harrity said.

I nodded.

"Explore what you need to," Harrity said, "and thank you for the update."

That was my dismissal. I picked up my notepad and shuffled out of his office.

13

That evening, Anna came over for a quick dinner before she went to work. Our meal was subdued, and we exchanged mundane details about our day. I held back talking about the specifics of the case I was on and she didn't share any of the patrol calls from her previous shift.

Sometimes, it was like this between us. A sense of quiet pervaded our time together. It wasn't distance, just a mutual, unspoken desire not to dive into those sometimes dirty, ugly, and complicated pieces of our work lives. There were other times when we shared extensively. Somehow, we could both sense which the other preferred. It was a comforting rhythm.

After she left for work, I tried to watch some television but couldn't concentrate on what was occurring on screen. Finally, I flicked it off and sat in the quiet of my small house thinking of Laura. I pulled her photograph from the file and peered down at it. Her kind and vibrant smile stared back up at me. The sense I got from her was one of warmth. It was inviting. That smile made me want to know her.

"Where are you?" I muttered.

More to the point, *how* was she?

Competing images sprang to mind. Laura holed up in a cheap motel, miserable and scared. On the heels of that, a vision of her moldering in the ground. Both clashed with the beaming woman stepping out of the kitchen, looking almost like a ballerina in her bridesmaid dress. So, I conjured up a scene of Laura sitting on a beach somewhere, sipping a victory cocktail.

That one didn't fit, either. Beautiful smile or not — kind person or not — Laura Shelton was a thief who had been stealing money for a decade before she disappeared. Did she really deserve to be on a beach somewhere?

It was a question I had no answer to, but that didn't stop me from dwelling on it and others until I was eventually tired enough to put her photo away and collapse into bed for a dreamless sleep.

14

The next morning, I arrived at Fresh Pines Cleaning bright and early. The doors were still locked. I stood out front, sipping from a coffee I'd bought from one of the scores of drive-through coffee stalls littered throughout River City.

I glanced at my watch: 7:50. As Ted pointed out to me yesterday, the sign said the office opened at eight and, based on what he said, I would have expected employees to actually be inside earlier than that. However, when I tapped my key on the glass window pane in the door, I got no answer.

I settled in to wait.

A couple of minutes later, I heard the squeal of hinges and the ding of a bell as the door to the Hillyard Barber Shop opened. Ted stepped outside holding a cigarette pack and a lighter in his hand. He saw me. After a moment, recognition registered in his eyes.

"Back again, eh?" Ted tapped out a cigarette and put it between his lips.

"No," I said. "I'm actually just here to watch you smoke."

Ted grinned and lit the cigarette. He took a drag and blew it out the side of his mouth. I don't know why the first, brief scent of a cigarette is different than what comes after, but it is. I always liked it, even though I came to despise the usual smell that followed.

"Any luck locating Laura?" Ted asked. He tried to sound casual, but I could hear the curiosity in his voice. Something else, too.

Concern.

"How'd you know I was looking for her?" I asked.

Ted shrugged. "I hear things. People talk. Especially at a barber shop."

"Well, I'm not really able to say—"

"I hope you find her," Ted interrupted. He took another deep drag on the cigarette and sent it billowing upward. "Laura is a sweet girl."

"You said that before," I said.

He shrugged. "It's true, that's all."

"She's forty-something," I said. "Hardly a girl anymore."

"Forty-four," Ted said.

I raised a brow. "She's forty-four?"

He nodded. "She had a birthday last month."

Why did he know that? I glanced up at the sign to his barber shop. Somehow, I didn't see Laura getting her hair done there.

Ted must have noticed my expression. "She's a smoker, too," he explained. "Occasionally, we'd end up on a break at the same time. We talked."

"I see." I motioned to the sidewalk where we stood. "Out here?"

"Off-hours, yeah," he said, nodding. "Or if things were slow. Most of the time, we'd smoke out back."

"What'd you two talk about?"

Ted shrugged. "Your typical stuff. How our day was going. Events. Plans. Life, basically."

"When was the last time you saw her?"

"Oh, man." Ted glanced up in thought. His cheeks puffed out and he let a long breath escape while he considered my question. "A day or two before she disappeared, I guess."

"Did you get the sense anything was amiss with her?"

"Amiss?" He cocked his head. "Like what?"

"That's what I'm asking. Did she seem different to you? More worried, or withdrawn?"

"Not that I remember." He paused for a moment, clearly deciding whether or not to continue.

"What is it?" I prompted. "Anything might help."

"I don't know how this would," said Ted. "I mentioned her birthday before. Last month?"

I nodded, and motioned for him to continue.

"Well, her husband forgot."

"He forgot her birthday?"

"Completely and utterly."

"So, like, a day late, or…?"

"Nope," said Ted. "Came and went and he never

mentioned it. It was like it didn't even exist."

"Was she upset?"

"She was hurt." Ted glanced at me then took a drag on his cigarette. "It seemed like it, anyway," he added as he blew it out. "I mean, that's pretty lousy, isn't it? Forgetting your own wife's birthday?"

"It's not good," I agreed. "Are you married?"

Ted shook his head. "Divorced about six years ago. She was a hard person to like, but I'll tell you this—I never forgot her birthday *or* our anniversary. That's just basic courtesy."

I shifted the subject. "Did she ever talk about working here?"

"Sure, we talked shop a lot."

"Did she like it?"

Ted pursed his lips. "I think so. I mean, accounting isn't exactly a dream job, is it?"

"What was her dream job?"

"That's the funny part," said Ted. "Her dream was to become a partner in the business."

A small jolt of interest zipped through me. "Partner, huh?"

Ted nodded. "That's what she said."

"When did that idea start?"

"I'm not sure. I don't think it's the job she fantasized about as a little girl or anything but, for years now, it's what she said she wanted."

"That didn't happen."

Ted shrugged and took a final drag of his cigarette. Then he stubbed it out on the bottom of his shoe and slipped the butt into his pocket. Finally, he looked back at me, his expression pained. "That's the way with most dreams, isn't it?"

When I didn't answer, Ted turned away and went back inside his barber shop.

15

Five minutes later, Rena Pines arrived.

She wasn't alone. A muscular man with short brown hair trailed behind her. He wore tight jeans and an even tighter black T-Shirt that looked at least one size too small. His broad chest pushed against the material and the sleeves bit into his biceps.

Rena scowled when she saw me. "What do you want?"

"I wanted to talk to your father again."

"Well, he's not here," she said. She dug into her purse and pulled out a ring of keys. As she unlocked the front door, she glanced over at me. "Why are you still here?"

"I'm waiting for your father to show up."

She sniffed. "You'll be here a while, then. He's at his doctor appointment."

I raised a brow. "Everything okay?"

Her scowl deepened. "None of your business."

The man behind her edged forward a half step, puffing out his chest and holding his arms out to his side slightly, looking as if he were holding an invisible bucket in each hand.

Classic macho peacock behavior, I thought.

I ignored him and kept my focus on Rena as she pushed open the front door. "Maybe you and I could talk?"

"About what?"

"I'm not entirely sure," I admitted. "Anything might help me find her."

Rena shook her head. "Listen, I've got nothing to say about that bitch. We trusted her and she betrayed us. Now, my dad can't retire for years."

"If I can find her, it might be possible to recover some of the stolen money."

"Ha!" Rena scoffed. "What dream world do you live in? That money's gone."

"Maybe," I admitted. "But maybe not."

Rena glanced at her companion, then back to me. "Here's a maybe for you, mister. *Maybe* Laura better hope I never find her. Between Tyler and me, we will get our money's worth out of her useless hide."

Next to her, Tyler grinned malevolently and jutted his jaw outward. Confidence radiated from him like a bad stench.

Rena glowered at me. "Now, unless you've got some office space you want to hire us to clean, get out of my face."

16

I found Kitty's Koffee Korner easily enough. Not surprisingly, it was located on a large corner lot on Monroe Street. The small rectangular building sat away from the street, with a drive-thru lane alongside. Parking spaces were available on both sides of the coffee shop.

Business was brisk inside, though the drive-thru only had one car in it. I had to park in the back.

Inside, the place had a casual vibe. All but one of the eight tables that lined the sides of the narrow building were full. Patrons sat chatting quietly. Some read or worked on a laptop. At one table, a man and a woman played chess.

At the counter, I was greeted by an attractive woman in her late twenties. She had big hair that made me think of a 1980s heavy metal video. Her name tag read Dania.

"What can I get you today?" she said, her tone lathered with business-nice.

"Is Missy around?"

"She'll be back in a moment. Can I help you?"

I ordered a black coffee.

"For here?" Dania asked, and I nodded. She grabbed a ceramic cup and filled it.

I took out my wallet and said, "I'm the guy Missy hired to find her sister."

Dania gave me a side-eye as she completed the fill. "You're a lawyer?" she asked, her disbelief plain.

I chuckled, though the sound felt somewhat forced even to my own ear. "No, I'm an investigator. I work for the lawyer."

"Oh." Dania plunked the cup onto the counter. Her gaze quickly swept up and down, taking me in. "That tracks," she said flatly.

She recited the cost of the coffee. I handed her a bill. "She said you encouraged her to go."

"Yeah, I did." She punched a few keys and the cash drawer of the register slid open.

"May I ask why?"

"To protect her interests," Dania said, withdrawing my change.

"What interests are those?"

"She's the sister. She has rights."

"Her sister is missing," I said. "What rights are you referring to?"

Dania extended her hand toward me. "Your change, sir."

I didn't accept the money right away. "I'm just trying to understand, that's all."

Dania lowered her hand and tilted her head. "Then catch a clue, mister. That Erik is a shit. I don't want my friend getting screwed over by him if…"

At that moment, I spotted Missy Jardin exit the bathroom. She wore a white shirt with the coffee shop's logo on it and a dark blue barista apron over a pair of jeans.

Dania glanced that direction and back to me. "You might be looking for the sister or whatever, but remember who hired you. Make sure you protect her." She held out her hand again.

As I accepted my change from Dania, Missy saw me. Her expression took on a worried note and she hurried over.

"Is everything all right?" she asked.

"It's fine," I assured her. "I was hoping we could talk for a few minutes."

Missy glanced at Dania, who shrugged. "I can cover, unless we get a rush."

Missy thanked her. We moved over toward the empty table and she stopped. "Would outside be better?" she asked. "For privacy?"

"Sure."

We stepped out onto the small patio, which faced the street. There were only three tables and all three were unoccupied. Missy sat at the nearest one and clasped her hands. "Are you sure everything's okay?"

"Why wouldn't it be?" I asked, sitting across from her. I took a sip of the dark brew and set it on the table.

"Because Laura's gone," Missy said. "I keep expecting bad news."

"I don't have any kind of news," I told her. "I

haven't found your sister yet."

"Oh." She looked both disappointed and relieved at the same time. "Then why are you here?"

"I don't think we got a chance to have a complete conversation yesterday at Harrity's office," I said. "So, I wanted to follow-up."

"All right. I don't know what else I can tell you."

"Did you have any idea Laura was stealing money from her employer?"

Missy shook her head. "Not a clue. I figured she just made good money." She motioned at the coffee shop. "Most of my jobs have been like this one. Laura was a professional accountant, so it made sense to me she did well for herself."

"She usually paid, you said? Whenever the two of you went out for lunch or whatever?"

"Always," Missy said. "It got to the point where it wasn't even a question."

"Was this something she'd always done? Or more recently?"

Missy thought about it. "She did it a lot when I was a kid. Maybe not so much once I started working if I remember. Could have been I was excited to pay. Show her I was grown up, you know?"

I nodded.

"Anyway," Missy said, "over the past ten years or so, she's mostly been paying again. Probably she thought I didn't make much money working here. It's barely above minimum wage but the tips make up for it." She peered more closely at me. "Why do you ask?"

"Just getting an idea of your relationship," I assured her. "Any thoughts on where she might have gone?"

"No."

"She never talked about a place she wanted to escape to or…?"

"No," Missy repeated. "That's part of what surprised me so much about all of this. She seemed like she was happy with her life."

"How about her marriage?"

Missy tilted her head and swallowed. "What do you mean?"

"Was her marriage a happy one?"

Missy wet her lips. She took a deep breath and let it out. "I mean… I think every marriage has, like, its ups and downs. She and Erik might have been in a down spell recently."

"How recently?"

"The last year or so, I guess."

"What did Laura say to make you think that?"

"Little things. Side comments, really. How Erik didn't pay attention to her or how he'd rather be off playing hockey or whatever." She twisted her lips to the side and bit the bottom one. "I don't know if she was being entirely fair, though. I mean, it takes two, right?"

"It does. Did she ever talk to you about Erik having an affair?"

Missy's eyes flared slightly. "An aff… *really?*"

"You didn't know?"

She shook her head wordlessly.

"Laura never said anything?"

"No," Missy said. She leaned forward. "Are you sure?"

"I am."

"How do you know?"

"Apparently, it's common knowledge amongst his friends," I said.

"Do you know who the woman is?" Missy asked, leaning forward slightly.

"A bartender," I told her. "If gossip is to be believed, anyway."

"A bartender," Missy repeated, her voice soft. She leaned back and repeated, "A *bartender*."

"Laura never talked about it?" I asked. "Never mentioned any suspicion, or…?"

"Never," she breathed. "I would have remembered that."

"Erik told me they had an understanding."

"An under…" A shadow of confusion filled her eyes, then melted into anger. She set her jaw. "That *prick*."

"So, he lied about that?"

"I don't know," Missy admitted, her eyes still alight with anger. "But I don't believe it. Not only would she never agree to something like that but, if that were true, Laura would have told me about it."

"That makes sense," I said. "Let me ask you something else—did Laura have any friends that might hide her if she ran?"

Missy's response was immediate. "No, she

didn't really have many friends at all. Laura was a loner. I don't think she chose to be, but she was a workaholic, you know? So that pretty much meant no real friends."

"Except you."

Missy spread her hands. "That's what sisters are for. When we were kids, it was mostly Laura taking care of me, more like a mom than a sister. Once I grew up, things shifted some. We got close in another way. More like equals, you know?"

"I understand." I thought for a second, lifting my coffee cup but not drinking right away. "Could Laura have gone to your parents?"

Missy scoffed. "Not likely. Mom died three years ago."

"I'm sorry."

She lifted a shoulder in a bare shrug. "It's sad, but it was a long time coming. She was a heavy drinker."

Missy looked over at the drive-thru lane that curved around the side of the building. The tail end of a car was angled at the corner. "I have to go soon," she said. "That's probably the fourth car in line. Dania will need my help."

"Okay," I said. "We're almost finished. What about your father?"

"We haven't heard from him for at least ten years now."

"Any idea where he might be?"

"Last I heard, he was bouncing at some cowboy bar in Tucson. The way he flitted from job to job, he's probably had twenty others since then."

"What's his name?"

"Devore," she said, "but he went by Buck."

"Did Laura have any sort of relationship with her father?"

"No more than I did. He was in and out of our lives when I was in grade school, and then rarely after that. I think I was a sophomore the last time I actually saw him in person. He called a few times but, like I said, it's been at least ten years." She frowned. "He could be dead by now for all I know."

The gravity of her words must have struck her, because a moment later, her eyes sparkled with tears.

"Oh God, so could Laura, couldn't she?"

"I don't know," I said honestly. "I haven't seen anything to indicate that."

She took a paper napkin from her apron pocket and dabbed at her eyes. "I keep thinking how much I want to know she's okay. Then I realize, no matter what you find out, it won't be okay, will it? She'll either be in trouble or hurt. So, I'm in this strange place. I want to know but I'm afraid to know. Does that make sense?"

"It makes perfect sense."

Missy took a deep, wavering breath and blew it out. Then she glanced over at me. "Erik was really seeing some bartender?" she asked.

I shrugged. "That's what I've been told."

She swallowed thickly. Her eyes darted away then returned to meet mine. "You don't think he…"

She let the idea die on her lips.

"I don't know," I answered. "I'm still trying to get a handle on the situation. The police don't seem to think so."

Missy took in the information, a hint of relief crossing her face. "They'd know, right? If he hurt her, I mean."

"Usually," I said.

I watched while she dabbed at her eyes again.

"Missy, is there something more you want to tell me?"

She didn't meet my gaze. "No," she said, her voice heavy with more threatening tears. "I'm just worried about her and I don't know what to think."

"What does your gut tell you?"

Missy's face contorted briefly, as if she were about to sob, but she fought it off. After a moment, she regained most of her composure and turned back to me. "My gut tells me no one else is looking for her, so you're her only chance," she said. "So, please… find my sister?"

"I'll do my best," I said, and I meant it.

17

After talking with Missy, I sat and finished my coffee. Dania's statement about Erik blended well with my own assessment of the man. I couldn't say what Missy's "rights" might be when it came to Laura and any of her assets, but didn't disagree with Dania's assessment. If Erik had the opportunity, he would certainly look out for number one.

I left Kitty's Koffee Korner and made my way back to my car. As soon as I rounded the rear of the vehicle, I saw the long gouge in the paint. It ran from the rear quarter-panel all the way to the middle of the driver's door. The work had been done with either a key or a small screwdriver.

Tiny flecks of paint clung to the narrow band of damage, attesting to how fresh it was. Whoever did this managed to pull it off while I was sitting with Missy on the opposite side of the small building.

I wondered why someone might do this. It could simply be random vandalism, I supposed. Or maybe the person in the next stall didn't care for my parking job. My Celica isn't a big car and it was positioned well within the painted lines on the asphalt.

When I reached the door, I spotted a slip of paper tucked under the windshield wiper. I lifted the wiper and picked up the note. "Fuck Off!" was written in hastily scrawled block letters.

I glanced around to see if anyone was watching me. No one seemed to pay me any interest. Whoever had done this was long gone.

Random? I wondered again.

Somehow, I didn't think so.

I cast my gaze around the area, searching for security cameras. I spotted one at the corner of the coffee building, aimed directly at the drive up window. The angle wasn't good for catching someone in the parking spaces, unless it was a wide lens.

I slid the note into my pocket and trudged back inside. Missy gave me a questioning look when I entered. I motioned in the direction of the drive-through window.

"Does that camera see the parking stalls on the back side?" I asked.

Her expression was momentarily confused. "Why?"

I told her what happened. Her eyes flew up as I described the gouge along the side of my car.

"That's horrible."

"I have insurance," I said, though I didn't relish making a claim. I motioned again with my hand. "The camera?"

"Oh. Right." She shook her head sadly. "Sorry.

The angle is up tight to the window. Dania had some trouble with a guy one night a few months ago, so the owner adjusted the zoom so the license plate and the driver are clear."

I thanked her and left.

Par for the course.

I headed home for an early lunch and to inspect the damage to my car more closely. Using a soft cloth, I wiped across the gouge. Whoever did this made sure to press hard—the damage was all the way down to the frame. This was beyond using a little nail polish for a touch up.

Inside the house, I called Detective Dow again. She surprised me by answering her phone.

"I'd like to look at the credit check you ran," I said. "Did you seize any credit card statements?"

"I have both," Dow said, reluctantly.

"Could I get copies?"

"Why?"

"The same reason you seized them," I said. "It might help me find Laura Shelton."

Dow was silent on her end of the phone for a bit. Then she said, "Most people would need to do a public disclosure request to get that. You're really playing on my regard for Lawrence Pines here."

"I'm just asking for some professional courtesy."

"Are you serious?"

"I am. You're an investigator. I'm one, too. We want the same outcome."

"We may want the same outcome, but don't think that makes us the same."

I could feel Dow's coldness through the phone. The tone made my jaw clench. I'd been eating shit from the RCPD for a decade and a half. Most of the time, I took it because I figured I deserved it. There were days when it got old.

"Well, then, it's good our goals are aligned, isn't it?" I said briskly. "When can I come by and pick up those copies?"

Dow didn't answer for a moment. Then she said, "I'll leave them for you at the front desk. Come get them whenever you want."

"Thanks," I said.

"Anything else?"

I almost said no, but then something occurred to me. "Actually, there might be. Does your locate on Laura include her car?"

"Not anymore," said Dow. "We found her car a few days ago in a Walmart parking lot."

I shifted in my seat, wondering why she hadn't told me this before. "Who left it there?"

"We don't know. The cameras don't extend to the main arterial and none of the other cameras in the area are at an angle to cover it, either."

"Was there any evidence inside?"

"No sign of foul play, if that's what you mean. Her phone was in the glove box." Dow's voice remained tight and even. "No purse, though."

"Were the keys in it?"

"Yes."

"What do you make of that?"

Dow was quiet for a moment. Then she said, "If she's on the run and abandoning the car, she didn't need the keys, so she left them. If someone else dumped the car there, they didn't need the keys, either."

I thought about what she said. Was the lack of camera coverage incidental or did the person who left the car there know it was a dead zone and choose it purposefully?

"Anything else?" Dow repeated, her tone drifting toward impatient.

Another thought struck me. "One more. Did you happen to come across a guy named Tyler? He's Serena Pines's boyfriend, I'm guessing."

"What about him?"

"That's my question. What's his last name and his background?"

There was another pause while I guessed Dow considered whether to answer me. The laws around disclosing confidential or privileged information had tightened since the years I was on the job. Even then, what I was asking might technically be a violation. No one really cared back then, is all.

But now? Now, cops were losing their jobs over it.

Still, Dow had to look at me as an extension of her own investigation at this point. I knew she didn't like the idea, but it was essentially true. Anything I found might even be useful in getting her case reactivated. She could easily justify sharing information that might result in either solving a crime or preventing someone being hurt.

The question was, would she?

She gave me the answer a few moments later. "Tyler Driggs," she said. "He's got eight or so entries. A few of them are assaults."

"Bar fights, or…?"

"I can't say without pulling the reports. A couple of DVs with no charges filed. The one conviction was for second degree assault." She tapped a few keys. "Victim in that case was a guy named Arlen Keating. Driggs did less than a year so he served his time at county rather than prison."

"Anything else on Keating?"

A pause, a few key taps, and Dow answered. "Looks like he died of a suicide."

"When?" I had an image of Tyler Driggs forcing a situation to look like a suicide.

Dow dashed my idea on the rocks. "He killed himself while Driggs was still in jail if you're thinking he might have been responsible."

"Oh. Well, either way, seems like he's a violent dude."

"Looks like it. Why do you ask?"

"He was with Rena when I went to Fresh Pines this morning. He was… less than friendly."

"That sums up my experience with him," Dow said, "and the daughter, Rena, too, if you want the truth."

It struck me that Rena had every right to be angry about Laura's theft and the lack of any police progress. But I knew that sentiment wouldn't sit well with Dow. Instead, I said, "I'd think she'd be happy someone is working the case."

"You'd think that, wouldn't you?" She sighed slightly. "Her attitude always seemed to be that I wasn't doing enough, and not quickly enough for her, either."

"How'd she take it when you suspended the case?"

"I put it to her that we were waiting for a hit on the missing persons locate. She was less than enthused at the news."

"My feeling is she doesn't expect to get the money back, even if Laura is found."

"She's a realist, then. Hold on a second." There was the sound of muffled voices, so Dow must have covered the mouthpiece. Then she came back on and said, "I've got to go. Something's come up."

"Thanks for the help."

"I'll burn these copies before I leave," she said. Then she hung up without saying goodbye.

I slid my phone back into my pocket. Despite Dow's coolness, she represented some of the best cooperation I'd had with RCPD since I stopped being a cop.

In the kitchen, I took my time making and eating a sandwich. I wasn't overly hungry but wanted to give Dow time to finish the task she promised to do. When I finished, I went out to my car. I spotted the old man with a checkerboard — Mick — sitting alone, reading a book.

I gave him a wave.
He waved back.

18

Getting into the Public Safety Building was a chore. No matter the time of day, there was a line at the entrance that edged forward slowly to get through the security station. I made sure to bring the bare minimum with me — basically, my wallet and keys. I stood in the warm sun outside the glass doors, inching steadily closer to the entrance. Once I made it inside, I watched the three people in front of me go through the station. When my turn came, I dropped my wallet and keys into the plastic bowl and stepped up to the metal detector.

"I have a prosthetic," I told the security guard. "It usually sets off the alarm."

He nodded and waved me through. Sure enough, the metal detector wailed in protest. The guard motioned for me to step to the side. Without being told, I held my arms out to the side and waited while he used a wand to scan me. A tickle of irritation fluttered in my chest. You'd think I'd be used to this by now. Yet, I always rankled at the indignity of standing there with my arms splayed while some guy waved the device all along my body.

When the wand activated on my lower left leg, he asked, "All right if I push up the pants to visually inspect?"

"No problem," I said stiffly.

He quickly lifted my pant leg a few inches and verified I wasn't smuggling in a weapon. A moment later, he held the bowl containing my wallet and keys out to me. "Thanks for your cooperation."

I took my items without a word and headed toward the police front desk. As I walked, I dug inside my wallet. Whoever was staffing the desk would almost certainly require ID to pick up the packet Dow left for me. My basic investigator card was unlikely to pass muster, so I withdrew my driver's license instead.

The front desk of the police department was staffed daily with a police officer. In my time on the job, it was an assigned position, but Anna told me it subsequently turned into a rotating assignment. For continuity, a senior volunteer worked alongside the commissioned officer unlucky enough to draw desk duty that day. I had no idea who that might be. I half-heartedly hoped whoever it was might not know me. Since the position drew from officers on day shift, though, and that shift was full of veterans, my odds weren't good.

When I reached the short line at the front desk, I saw it was Officer Aaron Norris working. Norris had been on for several years before I started. I rarely worked with him directly but he and his partner, Virgil Gilliam, were among the officers on graveyard shift with a reputation for chasing women.

The last time I'd seen him had been several years ago, in the midst of investigating a murder case for Harrity. Our interaction had been brief, but it was one of the few I could say wasn't negative, even though I spent most of it in the back of his police cruiser, being driven to the station for questioning.

Now, standing behind the police counter, I could see the signs of age creeping up on Norris. His shortly cropped hair was graying at the temples. Light lines crinkled at the corners of his eyes. He remained tall and trim, still a figure that inspired some confidence.

He recognized me immediately. When he finished helping the woman in front of me, I stepped forward. Before I could even say hello, he lifted a manila envelope.

"You here for this?"

I nodded and held out my hand.

Norris gave me the envelope. His face bore a curious expression. "What's in it, if you don't mind me asking?"

"Just some financial papers; a credit check, card statements, that sort of thing. Why?"

He shrugged. "The detective didn't seem too thrilled about leaving it for you, that's all."

I smiled slightly. "I get that a lot."

"I'll bet."

"Not from you, though," I said.

"I'm just a great guy that way. Ask anyone." Norris met my gaze. "The last time I saw you, you were in handcuffs."

"I get that a lot, too."

Norris laughed at that, a short bark that disintegrated into a rueful chuckle. "I'll bet," he repeated. "For some reason, you just keep coming back for more. Why is that?"

"Stubborn, I guess."

"That's one word for it."

"What word would you use?"

Norris grinned. "Now, you're expecting me to say *stupid* or something, aren't you? I can tell by the look on your face."

"Let's say it wouldn't surprise me."

"Yeah, well, I told you last time what I'd call it. You don't remember?"

I thought back to our conversation with me in the back of the patrol car, him driving. It had been four years ago, so it took a few seconds to recall. Then it came to me.

"You said I had balls," I told him.

Norris touched his nose and then pointed at me. "There's not as much of that in this world as there used to be," he said, tapping the counter for emphasis. "Less and less every day."

I didn't know how to answer that. Since there were people waiting in line, I lifted the envelope and said, "Thanks for this."

"No problem."

I turned and left the Public Safety Building. As I

walked back to my car, I shook my head in mild surprise. In the immediate aftermath of my disgraceful departure from the police department, if someone had asked me who might show some mild support toward me a decade and half later, Aaron Norris wouldn't have been in my top fifty guesses.

Yesterday Viola from the Swinging Doors made me think of how people are strange. After picking up Dow's packet from Norris, I decided to up the ante.

People might be strange, but *life* is stranger.

<h1 align="center">19</h1>

Seated in my car, I gave the paperwork a quick perusal. I knew I'd tear it apart later at home, but I wanted to get a first impression.

Laura Shelton's credit check was unsurprising. Her score was on the high side of normal. She had no judgments or late payments. Most of her accounts listed Erik as a joint account-holder, further strengthening his case for being vulnerable to any lawsuit from Pines. The only real debt she had was their home and Erik's vehicle. Neither figure was out of the ordinary.

The credit report wasn't just clean; it was what I'd expect from someone whose career focus was financial. Cops tend to have good locks on their doors, fire fighters have extinguishers in the house, barbers have sharp scissors in the drawer, and accountants tend to keep their financial affairs in order.

No big shock there.

I wondered if she had any dummy accounts set up somewhere. The inner workings of fraud weren't something I was overly familiar with, but it seemed to me that Laura could have created a business as a front and then funneled money to it via false invoices. The problem with that was it left a visible paper trail. Her fingerprints would be all over the dummy business, too.

Come to think of it, opening a bank account would require identification and the use of her social security number. All of it seemed terribly simple and unlikely to hold up to scrutiny.

I frowned. That was the beauty of Laura being the sole bookkeeper, though, wasn't it? *She* was the only one to scrutinize the accounts. As long as she avoided giving anyone a reason to audit her work, even a simple ruse like the one I concocted might work.

Whatever her scheme, all the details would come out in the forensic audit. Unsnarling the financial particulars wasn't my job. Finding Laura Shelton was.

The credit card statements held little in the way of surprises, either. For starters, Laura only had three cards. One was for a department store and showed little activity—a few clothing purchases, from what I could tell. The other two, one a VISA and the other a Discover Card, had light usage, especially the latter. As I ran my finger down the list of charges, I saw nothing of interest. I switched over to the VISA and saw only a few more entries, even though this was a card that also had a cash-back feature.

All of the entries pre-dated her disappearance. I

didn't expect she'd be foolish enough to use her credit card if she was on the run, but, then again, people do some foolish things at times.

After one pass, I went through the entries again much more slowly. This time, I noticed a small pattern. Once or twice a week, Laura had charges at a place called Cawfee Tawk. The amount seemed like a lot for just one person, even if she ate lunch there. On the other hand, it seemed about right for two people, especially if it included coffee and a pastry. So, maybe Laura had a friend neither Missy nor Erik knew about.

The question was, what kind of friend? A confidante or a lover?

There was only one way to find out.

I'd never heard of Cawfee Tawk, so I flipped open my phone and called 411. As it rang in my ear, I wondered how much longer this service would be available. Already, most people carried around smartphones capable of finding this information on the Internet. Only Luddites like me still carried a flip phone.

A man answered and I told him I needed the number and address for the coffee shop. "One moment, please," he said, and I could hear keys clacking in the background. Then the sound cut off and a computer voice recited the information. I jotted it down and broke the connection.

It turned out Cawfee Tawk was on the north edge of River City, in a newer commercial area north of Magnesium Road. I wasn't even sure if it was still within city limits until I saw the street signs remained white with black lettering. The county used white lettering on a green background.

The inside of Cawfee Tawk was open and sprawling, with a coffee counter and small kitchen at the far end. Two- and four-top tables were interspersed with couches and overstuffed chairs throughout the floor. A pair of electric fireplaces provided ambiance to go along with the folksy guitar music playing over the speakers.

While the space was filled with customers, there was no line at the counter. Behind the counter stood a twenty-something male with blond dreadlocks and a T-Shirt featuring a band I'd never heard of. He gave me an expectant look as I approached. A loop of gold pierced his eyebrow.

"What can I get you?" he asked.

"What's your name?"

"Zach," he answered automatically.

I showed him the photograph of Laura. "Zach, this woman is missing," I said. "Do you recognize her?"

He leaned forward, squinting at the picture. Recognition sparked in his eyes. "Oh, yeah, I've seen her. She comes in every week."

"Alone?"

Zach tilted his head, glancing upward while he thought. "No," he said. "I'm pretty sure she was friends with the dog lady."

"Dog lady?"

"She rescues dogs or trains them or something."

"Do you know anything else about her?"

He shrugged. "Most of my conversations are in one and two sentence blasts, man. I learn a little something about people but not the whole story. That's the job."

"Do you know the dog lady's name?" I asked.

"Nope. I'm pretty sure she put a flyer up on our community board over there, though." He pointed. "Sorry. Best I can do."

I tucked away Laura's photograph. "Thanks, Zach. You've been very helpful."

"Cool." He motioned to the espresso machine. "You want a coffee? I pull a mean shot."

"I'm about coffeed out for the day."

Zach waved a dismissive hand. "No such thing, man. You just gotta switch it up, that's all."

I smiled and nodded my thanks. Then I headed to the bulletin board along the wall. It was a mosaic of business cards and flyers offering everything from legal advice to computer repair. I scanned the board for a solid minute before I spotted what I was looking for.

"Pawsome Pups!" the postcard-sized flyer read. A small brown puppy's head made up the logo, along with the tagline, "Train 'em young—they'll love you for it!"

I removed the card and examined it more closely. The contact information included the name "Abby Groves, CCPDT certified trainer" and a phone number. On the back, there was a thumbnail photo of a smiling woman and list of services she provided.

I jotted down the number. Then I pinned the card back to the corkboard and left.

20

"Hello?"

"Abby Groves?"

"Speaking," she said. "Who's this?"

"My name is Stefan Kopriva. I'm an investigator for Joel Harrity."

There was a pause. Then Abby said, "Okaaaaay…."

"I'm trying to find Laura Shelton," I told her.

Once again, Abby didn't answer right away. After a few seconds, she asked, "Why are you calling me?"

"You and Laura met for coffee once or twice a week," I said. "At Cawfee Tawk."

She was quiet, not admitting anything.

"I'm hoping you might know something that will help me find her," I said.

"I don't."

"Can we meet anyway?"

"Why? I just told you I don't know where Laura is."

"I appreciate that. You might be able to fill in other gaps. Besides, in my experience, people don't

118

always realize they know something that might be helpful."

More silence. Then Abby said, "You said you work for a lawyer?"

"Yes."

"Erik hired you?"

It was my turn to hesitate. Once again, I was faced with the question of client confidentiality. There was something in her tone that made me answer. "No. It was her sister, Missy."

"Missy, huh?"

"Does that surprise you?"

"No. Nothing people do surprises me anymore." A few beats passed. Then Abby said, "All right, I'll meet with you. It'll have to be tomorrow, though. I've got an open hour at eight in the morning."

"That'll work. Where?"

"Might as well make it Cawfee Tawk."

"I'll be there," I said.

21

After my call with Abby Groves, I drove home.

I needed to think. Aside from talking to Abby tomorrow, I didn't see another investigative avenue to pursue. Laura had vanished leaving behind her car and phone. There was no activity on her credit cards. She was either using cash or had gone to the considerable effort of setting up a false identity. I leaned heavily toward the former.

Seated at my kitchen table, I opened the file Kylie had given me. The contents were thin so reading through it once more took very little time. None of the existing facts jumped out at me with a new wrinkle.

I switched to the credit card statement and credit report once again, scouring through it line by line. Nothing stood out.

Eventually, I found myself staring down at the photograph of Laura and comparing it to the later, darker one Erik showed me on his phone.

Photos capture a single moment in time. They don't necessarily represent a constant state of being. Yet, the positive energy that beamed out from Laura in the first photograph was palpable. It was difficult to imagine it only represented a solitary moment. Perhaps she was just overjoyed for her sister. The way Missy described their relationship, Laura was almost a surrogate mother. It made sense she'd be happy for Missy. That smile could be a flash of joy in the middle of an otherwise difficult time. It didn't look that way to me though. It looked more like she was a happy person.

I compared that to the more recent photo Erik Shelton texted me. As happy as she appeared in the bridesmaid shot, she seemed at least that miserable in the other. Was that simply a moment in time? A bad day for a generally happy person? Or was it her constant state?

Which was the real Laura? Or were both of them the real her just at a different place in her life? If that was true, what had caused the change? Was it sudden or gradual?

I shifted back to the photo of her in the dress. As I stared down at her radiant smile, the most pressing question seemed to be whether any of those other questions mattered at all when it came to finding her. Especially if she wasn't hiding at all.

I slid the photograph back into the folder and closed it.

That night, Anna stopped by before work. I made tacos and we chatted. Unlike the previous night, we drifted into work details. She told me about a domestic violence call she went on. The neighbors called it in as an ongoing assault. When Anna and Hattie Mayer arrived on scene, they discovered what they were actually interrupting was some passionate love-making.

"They must have been embarrassed," I said, chuckling.

"The wife was. The husband just wanted us to leave so they could go back to what they were doing."

"Really? He didn't think he just landed in a porn movie?" I cocked my head and spoke in a stilted, fake sexy tone. "Are you going to have to... *search* me, officers?"

Anna grinned. "Stop."

"Bom chicka wow wow," I half-sang. "Oh, look, you brought handcuffs."

Anna's grin broadened. "Really. Stop while you're ahead."

"Head?" I asked and shook my shoulders in mock seduction.

Anna rolled her eyes. "One too many times to the well, Stef." She waved her hand. "Tell me about your day."

I sighed. "No porn sequences there," I said. "Though it seems my missing woman's husband was fooling around."

Anna raised a brow. I took some time to outline everything that had happened so far. She listened carefully, chewing thoughtfully on her taco while I spoke. When I'd finished, she said, "It sounds like a mess."

"It is," I admitted. "There's no definitive evidence, which leaves so many different possibilities. The husband is a trash individual, but the case detective doesn't think he's good for murder. The victim seems conflicted about pursuing the case criminally and only wants his money back. His daughter is livid and has an intimidating boyfriend who just entered my suspect pool. The only one who seems to care about Laura is her sister, and even she thought to hire an attorney."

"Nothing on the credit cards?"

"Nothing except old use which led me to her friend, the dog trainer." I shrugged. "That's the only viable lead I've got at the moment."

"So..." Anna said. "What do you have? An embezzlement? A missing person? A murder?"

"Exactly." I finished off a taco and shook my head. "These are the toughest cases, when part of the problem is figuring out exactly what kind of case it even is."

"You don't think their marriage was happy?" Anna asked.

"I doubt it. The last photo I saw of her, she looked pretty miserable. Nothing like in the one from a few years ago."

"She's been embezzling from this business for how long? A decade or so?"

I nodded. "Why?"

"Just trying to talk through it," Anna said. "One

thought I have is a happy person doesn't steal money for ten years. She might be a woman who saved up for years to get out of an unhappy marriage."

"I don't know if she's been unhappy for that long."

"The photo you described, can I see it?"

"Sure." I stood and retrieved the file. I handed her the five-by-seven of Laura Shelton. While Anna looked at it, I shifted slightly. I knew thinking Laura had a particular beauty to her wasn't akin to cheating on Anna, but the moment still made me uncomfortable.

She examined the photo for a while before handing it back. "She has a glow to her," Anna said. "You said this was the day of her sister's wedding, right?"

"Yes."

"A sister for whom she was also something of a surrogate mother."

"Also true. Why?"

Anna pressed her lips together in thought. Then she said, "It's entirely possible she was happy in that moment *and* still miserable in the rest of her life. If so, my theory she was planning to leave for a long time still holds up."

"What about the idea she might be dead?" I asked.

"Who would want to kill her?"

"The guy she stole money from. His daughter. Not to go all Dateline on you, but the husband is always a possibility, too. Not to mention the chance it was someone completely random."

Anna considered. "I know you can't rule it out until you find her alive, but think about each of those suspects, Stef. Did the old man really seem like the killing type?"

"No," I admitted. "But maybe in the moment, he was more about the wrath of God than His forgiveness."

"You said he sounded mostly heartbroken."

I thought about my brief interactions with Lawrence Pines. "He was," I conceded. "Then again, he was angry, too. Looking broken up over it would make for a great cover story."

"Maybe in a Lifetime movie. How about the daughter? Did she seem angry enough to take revenge on someone for something that didn't happen to her directly? In my experience, the threshold for that is considerably higher than when someone is injured themselves."

"True... but she seemed pretty wound up."

"Or that's her normal state of being," Anna countered.

"Just as likely," I admitted.

"Moving on, what does the husband gain if he kills her? What's his motivation?"

"I don't know. People have all sorts of strange ones that aren't easy to see on the surface."

"They do. But most of the time, in spousal murders, it's pretty simple. It comes down to money or sex. Or both. In this case, it sounds like she had the money."

"Maybe he killed her to get his hands on it," I said, giving voice to the thought I'd had at Harrity's office earlier in the day.

Anna considered. "Possible. He has an alibi, no?"

"He does."

She turned over her hands in a *there-you-go* gesture. "As for your random killer theory…"

"Yeah, I know. There's no accounting for random events."

"That said, it's usually not random. That doesn't rule out it might be something totally different than anyone suspects." Her expression grew thoughtful. "You know, I heard about a case we had like this about a year ago. I mean, not exactly the same, but similar."

"They say history never repeats itself, but it often rhymes," I said. "Maybe the same is true with cases. How was this one similar?"

"Well, this woman was in her twenties, not her forties, so that's different. Like your missing person, she just disappeared. The detective didn't know if she was hiding out or in a shallow grave somewhere."

"What happened?"

"Turns out she married a fireman and moved to Phoenix to escape a suffocating relationship with her mother."

I smiled knowingly. "That's why you're thinking Laura was saving up to leave her husband."

"Maybe. You said she took a quarter million dollars, right?"

"Or thereabouts."

"That's not exactly live forever money, is it?"

"It's *live okay for a long while* money, though. Especially if you're thrifty."

"How old was the embezzler?" Anna asked. "Forty-something? Even if she lived cheap, the money would run out by the time she hits fifty-something. Then what?"

"She could get a job. Supplement her nest egg with some new income."

"That would require a new identity," Anna said. Then she shrugged. "Which, admittedly, isn't exactly hard to obtain."

"She could work under the table, for cash."

"I suppose."

"Or maybe she went to some other country where the cost of living is low."

"If that's the case," Anna said, "then not only would she need to create a new identity but also acquire a passport under that identity."

"How hard is that? If she already has good identification—"

"Getting a passport is a whole other level of scrutiny. It's a felony to apply under a false identity. You're risking a lot when you could just go live in Mississippi instead."

I wondered how long someone could make it on the money Laura stole. Then another thought struck me. "Honestly, I don't know for certain if there's any money at all. Or, if there is, what the true amount is."

"What do you mean?"

"All I know is what Pines told the police. I haven't seen the books. The forensic audit isn't underway yet, so the true answer is a ways off." I glanced up at Anna. "Maybe Laura only stole a fraction of what they're claiming or nothing at all. The Pines could be working an insurance scam or something."

Anna turned down her lips. "If true, that's another sticky wicket." She shook her head. "This is why I'm going to stay in uniform for my entire career. Wading through the big muddy like this is no fun. Give me the uncertainty and chaos of patrol any time."

"You're not exactly helping," I complained good-naturedly.

"Am I supposed to be?" A slight grin touched the corners of her mouth. "Mostly, I thought I was just agreeing with you that your case is a mess."

22

I recognized Abby Groves from the thumbnail photo on her business card. However, her pleasant features were masked in suspicion when I sat down at the table across from her.

"Do you have some ID?" she asked. "So I know who I'm talking to?"

"Sure." I pulled out my homespun investigator's identification and a business card and slid them across the table.

Abby examined them skeptically, glancing up at my face and back to the ID. "This isn't state-issued," she said.

"It isn't," I agreed. "I'm not a licensed private investigator. I am an investigator for an attorney here in town."

She slid the documents back toward me. "That sounds shady."

I picked up the ID card but pushed the business card back to her, almost as if I was giving her change for a purchase. She left it there, untouched. "The state doesn't require a license," I told her, "as long as you don't misrepresent yourself as a licensed investigator. It's a fairly common practice not to bother with the P.I. license unless you're setting up your own business."

Abby frowned. "I train dogs for a living and *I* had to get a license."

I slipped my ID card back into my wallet and shrugged. "Who knows with the government?" Then I changed the subject. "I'm trying to find Laura Shelton. I'm hoping you can help with that."

Abby watched me for a few seconds, as if deliberating whether or not to help me. I knew she had to be leaning toward doing so or she wouldn't have agreed to meet me in the first place. I was just as sure our first few moments together represented some kind of a trust test.

I waited.

She took a deep breath and let it out, nodding slowly. "All right. Yes. I don't know what help I can be, but I'll try. What do you want to know?"

"Let's start with this," I said. "Do you know where Laura is now?"

Abby gave me a confused look. "Of course not. What kind of question is that?"

"I'm just exploring possibilities."

"You're accusing me?"

"No," I said. "I have to ask the obvious questions first. You're her friend. It's not a crazy thought you might know where she is now."

"Well, I don't," Abby said firmly. Then her features softened. "I wish I did, though. I'm worried about her."

"Worried in what way?"

"In every way." Abby shrugged. "That she's hurt or in trouble."

"She *is* in trouble," I said.

Abby frowned. "For what?'

I nodded. "Were you aware she was stealing from her employer?"

"No. In fact, I'm not sure I believe you. Laura was a good person."

"I think she was, too," I said, "but she definitely took money. You didn't know about it?"

"Of course not," Abby huffed. "I would have told her to stop."

"Would she have listened to you?"

Abby considered. "I think so, yes. She respected my opinion."

"How long have you known her?"

Abby glanced up at the ceiling, thinking. "About five years, I think."

"How'd you meet?"

Abby chuckled briefly. "That's the ironic part. I hired her to get my books up and running for my business. She set me up and helped out for the first six months until I was up to speed on the software and everything. After that, we stayed friends."

"Did you see her often?"

"A couple of times a week," Abby said. She twirled her finger in the air. "We met here for coffee and commiserated."

"About what?"

"Life," Abby answered immediately. "Getting

older. Work being hard. Having shitty husbands."

I raised a brow. "So, you'd say her marriage was unhappy?"

Abby let out another chuckle. "For the last year, I'd say it was pretty miserable."

"What was the problem?"

She eyed me carefully. "Why does that matter? If you're trying to hunt her down..."

"I'm trying to *find* her," I clarified.

Abby didn't answer. She lifted her cup of coffee and took a drink. When she'd replaced it, she said, "You're saying maybe she didn't run away?"

I spread my hands. "I'll be honest—I don't know. It's my job to keep an open mind until I have confirmed the facts."

Abby's gaze drilled into me. "If she didn't run away with the money, the only person I can think of who might hurt her is Erik. Is that what you believe happened?"

"Open mind," I reminded her. Then I leaned forward slightly and lowered my voice. "Do you think he's capable of that?"

Abby pressed her lips together in distaste. "He's a cheating bastard, that's for sure. Classic narcissist. But murder?" She shook her head. "I don't know about that."

"Did Laura know he was cheating on her?"

"She's always suspected, I think. She got proof about a year and half ago."

"What kind of proof?"

"A phone call from one of the women he fooled

around with."

"Do you know who?"

Abby shook her head. "She wouldn't say other than her first name was Angie. This Angie woman was going through some twelve-step program so she was trying to make amends." She paused and smirked. "Seems more like she was trying to make herself feel better if you ask me, but there it is."

"Did Laura confront Erik?"

"The same day," Abby said. "They had a huge fight about it. He denied everything, of course. He gaslighted the shit out of her about it."

"How so?"

"He claimed it was someone with an axe to grind, probably from work. An angry customer looking to get even or one of the other salesmen upset over a stolen sale who had his girlfriend call." Abby smirked. "Typical."

"They stayed together," I said. "Why do you think they did?"

Abby heaved a heavy sigh. She gave me an appraising look then said, "You look pretty close to my age. You turn forty yet?"

"Last year," I admitted.

"Then you know." Abby pursed her lips. "By the time you get to our age, you've made the choices you've made. Life becomes about learning how to live with those choices."

I didn't agree with her philosophy but knew instinctively arguing about it would do me no good. So, I asked, "Did Laura feel that way, too?"

"She was smart," Abby said. "She was a realist about how much runway we had left to make any sort of life. Starting over at our age? It wasn't going to happen. So, you make do."

"Make do how?"

"Find something happy in your life to focus on."

"Like dogs?" I asked.

Abby frowned. "Don't be that way. We don't know each other well enough for you to say something like that."

"I'm sorry," I said breezily. "I'm just trying to understand. You said the two of you commiserated over bad marriages. I took that to mean you had the same issues she did."

"My issues are none of your business," she said icily. Her eyes narrowed. "Are you *really* trying to find Laura or just looking to stir up shit?"

"I only want to find Laura." I shrugged. "Sometimes the shit gets stirred up in the process."

"Well leave me out of that part."

"All right."

"Are we done?"

"Almost," I said. "I realize you didn't know about the money Laura was stealing but looking back now, did you see any signs of it?"

Abby's suspicious expression took a few moments to soften. Then she gave some thought to my question. Finally, she shook her head. "No, other than the fact that she always insisted on paying for our coffee."

"She did that with her sister a lot, too."

"That sounds like Laura."

"Usually it was with cash," I said. "Here she used a credit card. Any idea why?"

Abby pointed to a sign near the register. ELECTRONIC PAYMENTS ONLY, it read.

"They don't take cash?" I asked, astonished.

"Nope."

"Why not?"

"I asked the manager that once," Abby said. "He said it was pretty hard to rob a place with no cash in the register."

I re-read the sign, still surprised at the policy. Then I turned back to Abby. "Did Laura have any other friends?"

"Not really."

"Did she ever talk about someplace she might like to go?"

Abby laughed. "Like Paris, you mean?"

"I'm just trying to get an idea where she might have gone."

"I really have no idea."

"All right. How about this — did Laura talk much about work?"

"Sometimes."

"Did she like it there?"

"I think she did at one time. Maybe not so much these past few years."

"What changed?"

Abby hesitated. "I'm starting to feel bad about telling you all of this about her."

"Why?"

"It just feels… wrong. Like I'm talking behind her back. Laura trusts me."

"Because you're her friend."

"Exactly."

"So be her friend — help find her."

"I don't want to betray our friendship. We told each other secrets and…" Abby leaned back and crossed her arms. "This was a mistake."

"The only mistake is not following through, Abby," I told her in an even tone. "Something you know might be key in helping me find her."

"Why? So she can go to jail?" Abby shook her head. "I'm not too keen on helping make that happen."

"It's a possibility," I admitted. "If she's on the run. What if she's not? What if someone has hurt her? You'd want her found then, right?"

Abby's resolve seemed to waver. "Yes," she admitted. "But you don't know that's what happened."

"Neither do you. I can tell you're holding back something about Laura. Whatever it is, it might help."

She didn't deny my assertion which might as well have been an admission. I sat in silence, knowing the next move had to be hers. Abby stared at me for a full thirty seconds. I wasn't sure what was going on behind her eyes but I could tell the gears were turning.

Finally, she dropped her hands to the table. "Fine, I'll tell you. What changed at work for her was she finally gave up hope of being made a partner in the business."

"Partner, huh?" My mind flashed back to my conversation with Ted, the barber.

"That was her goal," Abby said. "She already handled all of the books and knew all of the vendors. The extra work she put in went way above the salary they paid her. She considered those hours a sort of investment, almost a form of sweat equity. The old man kept putting her off. Finally, about three years ago, he told her it was never going to happen. It was a family business and would remain so. He offered her a raise but there was no way she'd be elevated to business partner."

"That upset Laura?"

"Hell, yes it did. She worked her backside off for that business. Way above and beyond. Without her, it wouldn't function. Probably wouldn't even stay afloat."

"I don't understand," I said. "She kept the books. How—"

"She didn't just keep the books," Abby interrupted. "She interacted with all the clients. All of them *loved* her. She was a big reason they kept clients and why they got new referrals."

"So she wasn't just the bookkeeper," I said. "She was…"

"Essentially the sales department, too," Abby finished. "The lifeblood of any business and the old man either didn't recognize that or he didn't care."

"Why not just quit?" I asked.

"Easy for you to say," scoffed Abby. "Laura didn't have a degree in accounting. She had a knack for it and got in with a small business on the ground floor. When the business grew, she kept the position because she was good at it. If she quit, she'd be competing with kids twenty years younger with accounting degrees who are willing to work for less. It wasn't a very attractive option."

"That's why she stuck it out," I said.

"Exactly. Same as her marriage."

I mulled it over in silence while Abby slowly spun her coffee cup on the tabletop. What she described certainly seemed like motivation to start embezzling money. There was even a self-righteous flair to it—"they don't appreciate me, so I'm going to at least get mine." Only one problem with that scenario: it didn't fit the timeline. She'd been stealing for far longer, or so Pines claimed.

"Did Laura *always* pay for your coffee?" I asked.

Abby knitted her brow. "I already told you that."

"I'm just confirming."

She spread her hands. "Yes, she always paid, outside of a few times I managed to get to the register first." She peered more closely at me. "Why?"

"It might tie in with something her sister said. When did you last see Laura?"

"The day before she disappeared. We had coffee here."

"Did she seem okay?"

"Okay?" Abby shrugged. "She seemed the same

as ever. Maybe a little extra tired."

"She didn't mention her work issues?"

"No."

"Looking back, does that surprise you? Since you two were close?"

She thought for a moment before answering. "No, I think maybe she wanted to protect me from whatever was going to happen. Especially if she saw it as inevitable."

I nodded that I understood. "This is helpful. What else can you tell me?"

Abby hesitated, watching me. Then she shook her head. "That's it."

I sensed she was holding something back, but it also felt like pushing wouldn't do any good. I made a mental note to come back around to her at a later date. Then I stood, motioning toward the still untouched business card of mine in front of her.

"If you think of anything else, please call," I said.

Abby glanced at the card and back to me, not answering.

"Thanks for helping me," I said. "When I find her, I'll call you with an update."

Her expression shifted. "*When?* Not *if?*"

I shrugged. "I try to be an optimist."

Abby smiled and I saw a hint of that beaming expression from the back of her business card. It was the same shine Laura had in the photo I'd borrowed from Erik.

"Believe it or not," Abby said, "so do I."

23

On the drive to Hillyard, I tried to reconcile the different sides of Laura Shelton. The joyous figure in the photograph I took for my file contrasted with the snapshot Erik texted me. The version Abby Groves described seemed to be somewhere in the middle, though leaning toward the latter of late.

A cheating partner was nothing new to hear about. I saw plenty of that behavior in my short stint as a police officer. My time working for Harrity had served up even more. It seemed to me the majority of relationships involved at least one unfaithful moment, but that was probably my own cynicism chiming in.

I considered how I'd feel if Anna cheated on me. It wasn't something I worried about—that just wasn't in her nature. The destruction of trust it'd cause would be devastating. I don't think it was something I'd ever be able to get past.

Even so, I tried to imagine Laura's situation. Hurt by Erik's infidelity, then fed a steady diet of his gaslighting, her trust in him had to be battered. Yet, she remained in the relationship.

It didn't take long to understand why her expression went from joyous to miserable in those two photographs. Unless the happy photo was the true anomaly and she was always miserable.

This thought didn't sit well with me. True, happy people don't tend to steal from their employers for years and years, but the description from Ted the barber belied her default state of being miserable.

Either way, discovering Erik's reported infidelity—and, to be fair, I only had hearsay to support this—wasn't the catalyst for her embezzlement. That behavior started years ago. So, something else was at play in this situation.

I just had no idea what.

When I arrived at Fresh Pines, the buzzer sounded as I swung open the door. An employee I hadn't met directed me back to the manager's office. Lawrence Pines sat at the desk, staring intently at the computer monitor. He glanced up when I knocked.

"Any news?" he asked.

I shook my head. "Still running down leads."

Pines frowned. "Doesn't seem like here at my office is the best place to be doing that," he muttered.

I ignored his comment. People often think they know how to conduct an investigation despite their own lack of experience. I'm betting those same people think they know better than cops and teachers and professional athletes, too. Right along with being excellent drivers and superb lovers.

"I'd like to take a look at some of the financial records," I said.

"Why?"

"To be thorough. You never know what might point me in the right direction when it comes to finding her," I paused, then added, "and maybe your money."

Pines eyed me for a few seconds then shook his head. "I'm not opening my books up to a stranger."

"At least show me how she managed to get away with stealing the money. I assume you use some sort of accounting system."

"Of course, we do."

"Manual or electronic?"

"I started out with physical accounting books but, once Laura came on, we switched over to software." His frown deepened. "Looking back, that might have been my biggest mistake."

"How so?" I motioned to the chair in front of his desk, silently asking permission to sit.

Pines's gaze tracked my gesture and he nodded distractedly. "In the old days, everything was written down on the page. If someone made a mistake or something had to be changed, it was obvious. The paper was even designed to show eraser marks. You could see at a glance if there'd been any edits."

"People make mistakes," I said.

"Of course, they do. This way, you saw where

those mistakes happened and how often. With any good bookkeeper, such mistakes were few and far between and easily explained. If you didn't like the explanation, you could always go to other records to confirm."

"Walk me through that, if you would."

Pines pressed his lips together. "Did you never balance a checkbook or something?"

"I did," I answered, though the truth was I'd rarely done so, and transitioned to debit cards and ATMs as soon as the technology shifted.

"Same idea," Pines told me. "If I see an erasure, I can pull the invoice to see if what's written there coincides with the edit. Of course, there's the edit itself. Does the math work? If both things check out, then what got erased was probably just human error. That happens but, like I said, not very often."

"You liked that system, it sounds like."

"I didn't care one way or the other. It was the system we had. Then software got cheaper and better and Laura talked me into springing for it." Pines shrugged. "Seemed like a good move at the time. She said it made her job easier, that's for sure. What I didn't realize was it made it easier for her to steal from me, too."

"Why? I'd think the software would make everything more accurate."

"You ever hear the term, garbage in, garbage out?"

I nodded. "You're saying she put in bad numbers?"

"You got it. Near as I can tell, she changed the amounts on certain invoices when she entered them into the software. Since everything looks clean on the screen—" he waved a hand at the monitor on his desk, "—there were no telltale erasure marks. I had no reason to pull the original invoices."

"Those aren't digital, too?"

"Nope." He pointed to two metal, three-drawer filing cabinets along the wall. "Physical copies, filed away."

"Any reason to pull those out and look at them?"

"Not really," Pines said. "Occasionally, a customer might have a problem or a question. Laura would most likely be the one who would deal with that. If it happened to be one of the accounts she skimmed from, she could always make the adjustment to the software to cover her tracks."

"And there'd be no erasure marks," I said.

"Exactly." Pines took a deep breath and let it out. "There are ways to trace everything she did. I could go back and pull the invoices and see if they don't match. It'll be time-consuming and expensive and the forensic auditors I hire will eventually do that anyway, so why bother now? Anyway, Laura had access and control to the whole financial system. She handled everything. The only time I paid much attention to the books was the monthly profit/loss report and then at the end of the year."

"Not at tax time?"

Pines snorted lightly. "Guess who prepared the taxes for my review?"

I nodded that I understood. "Anyone else have access to the software?"

"I did, of course," said Pines. "Though I rarely had cause to use it. Rena acted as backup whenever Laura was out sick or took vacation."

"So, it's safe to say your understanding of the finances was more of a thirty-thousand-foot view, not down in the weeds."

"Exactly. I focused on my clients and employees. Not having to deal with the daily details of the cash flow freed me up for that." Pines's frown returned. "Looking back, I gave her too much power. But I trusted her."

I thought of how Erik had broken Laura's trust and realized this wasn't much different. Money instead of sex, and still a betrayal.

"Why did you trust her?" I asked Pines.

"She was trustworthy," he said simply. "I would have left my grandkids with her if I had any. Laura was like a daughter to me."

"How'd you catch her?"

"That was Rena. She got suspicious and started digging."

"What made her suspicious?"

"Expensive perfume is what she told me." Pines shrugged. "It's a woman thing, I guess. I told her she was crazy, but then she found a couple of doctored invoices."

"Did you confront Laura?"

"Not right away. First, I had Rena do some more work so I could be sure it wasn't just a mistake. The more she dug into the records, the more it became undeniable." He sighed again, his expression laced with disappointment. "She'd been stealing from me for years."

"Fifteen, you said. That adds up to a lot of money."

"Two hundred fifty thousand," Pines agreed. "I told you this when you were here before. Why bring it up again?"

I shrugged. "Her husband guessed half a million."

"That goof?" Pines sniffed derisively. "He wouldn't know buckwheat from buckshot. No, Rena did some rough math and I trust her estimate."

"Still a lot," I said.

He drummed his fingers on the desk. "It adds up, over time. You heard Rena say it: my retirement fund would be significantly bigger if the money went there instead of into her pocket."

"It sounds like she stole it in dribs and drabs."

"Dribs and drabs?" Pines frowned at the words. "I'd say it was more like a steady trickle. A few hundred every week. More, the longer she got away with it."

"Now that you've stopped the bleeding, profit should get better."

"You'd think so. Except once the auditors figure out how much she stole, I have to pay taxes on it." He shook his head. "You'd think being a fraud victim would get some sympathy from the IRS, but they couldn't care less, the jackals. Fresh meat or lost meat found rotting on the bone, they still want their taste."

I shifted in my seat. "Her husband said something about her wanting to become a partner in the business?"

The frown that creased Pines's face deepened into furrows. "Same husband who said it was half a million? What does he know?"

I turned up my hands. "She didn't talk partnership to you?"

Pines exhaled and nodded. "Yeah, she started bringing it up about five years ago. Why does that matter?"

"I don't know if it does. But that's the point—you never know what matters. That's why I ask a lot of questions."

"Well, you've got that part down," Pines groused. He rubbed his mouth then said, "I put her off. She didn't ask again for a few years. Then she brought it up sometime last year."

"What'd you tell her?"

"I told her no," Pines said. "This is a family business. As much as I treated her like a daughter, she wasn't my blood. The business will go to Rena when I retire. Besides, I didn't need or want any partners."

"Wouldn't she have to buy in or something anyway?"

"We didn't get that far in the discussion," said Pines. "But yeah, there'd need to be something more than her being a loyal employee." He scoffed at that then added, "If I'd said yes, I guess she'd be buying her way in with the same money she stole from me. That's what people mean when they say ironic, don't you think?"

I spread my hands. "She made that offer?"

"No. Like I said, we never got that far in the conversation. She brought up how long she'd worked for me and how important she was to the business. I said both of those were true, but neither one made her a partner."

"Do you think she resented you for that?"

"She might have," Pines admitted. "I would've." He shrugged. "Heck, maybe she did deserve to be brought in, with all she did. Or a raise, at least." His eyes shone with anger. "But to steal from me? That's wrong, no matter how you look at it."

Pines now seemed more angry than heartbroken, and I supposed it was understandable. When someone breaks a person's trust, the reaction isn't only one emotion. This was a fifteen-year relationship Laura betrayed.

"I'm sorry," I said, not knowing what else to say.

Pines cleared his throat. "We're all sorry. I'm sorry to be so harsh or to speak ill of her husband. It's not very Christian, is it? But, like I said, we all disappoint." He gave his head a short shake. "Anyway, do you think you'll find her? The cop on the case seems to have given up."

"I don't think she has," I said. "When I talked to her, she was still looking at options."

Pines smirked. "She's a government employee.

In my experience, the only option they look at is how to avoid more work. Perhaps I'm wrong." He leaned forward. "My question is, are *you* going to find her?"

"I'm going to try."

"Try, huh?" Pines looked dubious. "That doesn't sound too promising."

"I don't like to make guarantees unless I know I can deliver."

There was a chuffing sound from behind me. Pines looked up and I turned to see who it was.

Rena Pines stood in the doorway, her eyes narrowed in suspicion. Tyler Driggs loomed over her shoulder giving me a sour look.

"What's going on here, Dad?"

Pines waved a hand. "Just talk." His gaze flicked back to me. "Probably all it will add up to, most likely."

I didn't bother telling him that most of my work as an investigator involved talking.

"Are you still looking for that bitch?" Rena growled. "You ought to be down in Mexico or something, not bothering my dad about it."

I took my cue and rose. "Thanks for your help, Mr. Pines."

He grunted in reply.

I turned and walked toward the door. When I reached it, Rena hesitated before stepping aside. Tyler took even longer to make way for me to leave. His intimidating scowl radiated toward me as if the man were perpetually angry.

When he finally moved, I made my way toward the front of the store.

"Mexico!" Rena Pines called after me.

24

Ted the barber waved to me again as I passed his shop on the way to my car. I waved back, distracted. Rena Pines and Tyler Driggs were on my mind. More specifically, her attitude and his propensity for violence.

I got into my car and pulled out of the parking spot. I drove around the block, stopping up the street so I could see the Fresh Pines storefront. I turned off the engine and waited, thinking.

It was entirely possible Laura Shelton was still alive. She could be hiding somewhere, spending the cash she stole. The longer I dug into this case, the more I was beginning to worry she was dead. Erik was my first suspect, though pinning down his exact motivation for killing his wife was anyone's guess. Did she confront him about his affairs? Threaten to divorce him? Had he discovered the embezzlement and wanted to keep the proceeds for himself?

Any of it was a reach, at least factually. The vagaries of human behavior, though? Anything was possible there.

Which brought me to Rena Pines and Tyler Driggs.

If Laura had been murdered, could one or both of them have done it?

Rena certainly had motive to do so. Laura's theft alone might be enough. I didn't know how much damage the losses did to the business, but she had said it prevented her father from retiring. Rena didn't hide how angry it made her. Could there be more?

I thought of how Lawrence referred to Laura as being like a daughter to him. He already had a daughter. I could see how his comments might breed jealousy and resentment in Rena. Maybe not enough to kill Laura, at least, not until you threw in the embezzlement. Might that be enough to push Rena over the top?

I had no idea. Rena was angry, that much was clear. Still, I didn't know her baseline. Perhaps she was angry all the time. Murdering someone might be way outside her wheelhouse.

But Tyler Driggs? He might be a different story.

Admittedly, his record only included assaults, not murder. Violence was violence, though, and he'd shown himself capable of it. If he loved Rena and she asked him to hurt Laura for what she did… would he?

Again, I didn't know. My gut said he would, but it was also entirely possible I was looking for certainties to help offset this constant feeling of not knowing that had been in play since I first took this case.

I remained in the car, continuing to wait. The truth was, there didn't seem to be much else I could do at this point.

Forty minutes later, Tyler Driggs left the store. He was alone, which was what I'd hoped. The big man loped confidently down the sidewalk for most of a block, before getting into a late '70s Dodge Charger. Even from nearly a block away, I heard the guttural roar when he started the engine and revved it. Then he pulled away from the curb.

I followed.

Tyler drove like his personality—rude and aggressive. He accelerated and braked hard. At a yellow light, he gunned the engine to beat the red. I missed the light and caught up with him at the next light, which only highlighted how ineffective his style of driving actually was. Even so, he didn't let up. He jockeyed for position constantly and cut into spaces in traffic just barely large enough for his vehicle. The few times anyone protested with a horn beep, he answered with a middle finger.

I shadowed him across the north side of River City until he stopped at a sporting goods store. There, he spent about twenty minutes inside before exiting with a small bag. After that, he drove through a Taco Bell. While he waited in the long line at the drive-thru, I found a spot up the street to park and wait. My own stomach grumbled but I ignored it.

Tyler ate while he drove, heading south and then east. My interest piqued as we approached the East Sprague corridor, an area notorious for illicit drug trade and prostitution. An outlaw motorcycle gang had its clubhouse on the fringes of the Corridor, as well. I thought maybe my hunch to follow Tyler might bear fruit.

He turned off Sprague and parked in a small parking lot behind several businesses. I cruised slowly past, watching from the street as he exited his car and slung a gym bag over his shoulder. He strode jauntily toward the back door of one of the businesses. The sign above the door read *River City Boxing/Kick-boxing Club*.

I frowned.

His membership tracked with his personality, at least in the sense that he was violent in nature. Though, if I were being honest, it seemed a little too formal for how I pegged him. He seemed like the quintessential bad boy and those types didn't tend to be joiners, unless it was a frat house or a criminal gang.

I risked going through a drive-thru myself, getting a cheeseburger from the Zip's Burgers up the street, before returning and sitting off to watch Tyler's car and await his return. An hour and a half later, a sweaty Tyler emerged from the back door of the boxing gym. He still had some jump to his step. Those pre-workout tacos must have done the job.

Tyler's driving didn't improve as he headed

north again. Usually tailing someone involves finding the sweet spot between keeping distance to avoid suspicion and keeping the target in sight so as not to lose them. The challenge in following Tyler was to keep up with him while not driving in the same aggressive fashion.

It wasn't easy and I was on the receiving end of a middle finger twice before we reached a residential neighborhood just above Illinois Avenue. Tyler continued to Euclid, where he turned right and then almost immediately into a small apartment complex. I estimated about twenty units of squat four-plex buildings surrounded the parking area. Nothing to rival the ones further north that approached the size of small towns. These were older, and likely less expensive, too.

I stopped along the curb as Tyler found a parking space and went inside apartment seven. I noted the unit number and settled in to wait. There was no way to know if he was stopping off for a quick shower or would stay for a while. I realized I didn't know much of anything about Tyler Driggs — where, or if, he worked, how long he and Rena had been together, or what a typical day looked like for him. I didn't even know if this was his actual home. I made a note to do some further background on the man.

The next two hours went by as slow as time could possibly pass. Cars zoomed by my location. A few pedestrians walked past. A few people came and went from the apartment complex but Tyler's door remained shut. I started to wonder if he'd decided to take a nap or something.

In the third hour, my phone buzzed. I didn't recognize the number, so I answered with a simple, "Hello?"

"Yeah, this is Oliver Santos." His voice was guarded. "You left me a message about Erik Shelton."

Recollection flooded me. Santos was the one who vouched for Erik and his buddies to get on the hockey team.

"Thanks for calling me back," I said.

"I figure, when the cops call, you call back."

I hesitated. I'd identified myself as an investigator when I left Santos a message. He'd clearly jumped to the conclusion I meant police. Presenting myself as law enforcement was a huge violation — a crime, actually — but there was nothing that said I had to correct someone's misunderstanding.

I forged ahead, ignoring his comment. "Harper said you brought Erik and the other two aboard the team?"

"That's right."

"You work with them?"

"I mean… we work at the same place."

"Together?"

"No. Erik and the others are salesmen. I work in the body shop."

"So, would you say you're friends with Erik?"

"I guess." The reluctance in Santos's tone

remained.

"He's not in any trouble," I assured him. "I'm just trying to get a complete picture of the situation. It will help me find Laura."

Santos didn't answer.

"I don't want to take up too much of your time," I continued, "so I'll get right to it. Harper told me all three of those guys liked to chase women."

"Oh, yeah," Santos agreed. "It was their other sport besides hockey."

"Erik, too?"

"Him most of all." He paused, then asked, "Why does that matter?"

"Just filling out the picture," I said. "It helps to know where everyone was and who they were with when Laura went missing."

"Like, an alibi, you mean?"

"Exactly like that. Do you know the women Erik was seeing?"

"A couple of them, yeah."

"Who were they?"

Santos hesitated. "You're sure Erik's not in trouble or nothing? Because he's tight with the dealership manager. If he gets slammed over something I told you…"

"He won't. In fact, your information is more likely to strengthen his alibi."

Santos remained silent for a few seconds. Finally, he said, "All right. I know he was seeing Hailey, over at the Doors."

I already knew that. "Anyone else?"

"Stacia, at least for a while."

"Do you know where Stacia works?"

"I don't know if she has a day job. She runs the scoreboard clock and keeps the score sheet for the rec league games at night and for the over-fifty league which plays during the day." He paused. "I guess maybe scorekeeper *is* her day job."

I jotted down the information. "Anyone else?"

"I mean, there were plenty of others, believe that. Those are the only two I know."

I thanked him. Santos still sounded like he'd just done an undesirable job when he said goodbye, as if he'd managed to clean out the restrooms but still wasn't happy about it.

I waited until the third hour was up before I decided to call the stakeout. In addition to some background work on Tyler, I wanted to talk to Stacia.

I drove to the hockey rink. Inside, the door to the rink manager's office was closed and the lights inside were off. I wandered over to the snack bar. A woman in her forties watched me from behind the counter. I smiled at her and ordered a coffee. As she was withdrawing my change from the register, I asked her if Stacia was working today.

"Why?"

"I was told she works here. Is that wrong?"

She shook her head slightly. "No, she works the adult rec league games. Those are at night."

"What nights do they play?" I asked.

She eyed me suspiciously. "It's too late to join.

The season is underway."

"I thought I might come watch."

"Watch Stacia, sounds more like." She dropped the coins into my hand. Then she pointed across the lobby. "Schedule's on the wall."

I wandered over and examined the schedule while sipping my coffee. There were games from five-thirty until ten each night for the next three days in a row. I looked to see if the timekeeper was noted but all I saw were team names. I found Doc's Muffler Clinic scheduled for tomorrow night. I figured, if Erik had been seeing Stacia, she probably managed the scoreboard for the division he played in. Maybe she covered the others, too, but my best bet was to catch her tomorrow. Just to be safe, I jotted down the times for the over-fifty league as well. There were several in the daytime over the next few days.

After I jotted down the game times, I left the ice rink. I waved and smiled at the woman from the snack bar, but she only stared back at me with a suspicious glare. I wondered if I needed to adjust my interview style or something. I was being met with more and more suspicion lately.

25

At home, I spent some time doing what research I could on Tyler Driggs. I was unable to find any employment for him, but that didn't mean he didn't have a job. As much as things seemed to be trending toward information being online, the personal variety seemed mostly restricted to what people voluntarily shared. I wondered if that would change in the years to come. While that might make my job easier, I didn't welcome the loss of personal privacy.

Eventually, I ran out of investigative avenues on Tyler. Then I remembered something Missy said and typed "Buck Jardin" into the search engine. A return showed an obituary from an Albuquerque newspaper. The brief text stated Devore "Buck" Jardin had died over two years ago. There weren't any accompanying news stories with further details on the death itself. The obituary was sparse, not even listing surviving family.

I wondered if Missy knew. Somehow, I doubted it. I didn't want to be the one to tell her.

My thoughts drifted to the death of my mother around the same time. I hadn't seen her for years prior to that. She came back into my life with poor intentions, broke my heart for the last time, and ended up murdered. My emotions were still a little raw whenever I thought of her.

In a way, I had something in common with Missy and Laura. Before she died, my mother shared another nugget of news — my own father's death. He'd been out of my life even more completely than she had and yet, hearing of his passing struck a chord in me that still resonated two years later. It raised questions that, if they didn't go away, would need to be answered.

I imagined it would be the same for Missy and Laura, if I found her.

Since my mind wouldn't be quiet, I took to pacing through my house. It wasn't something I did enough to call a habit, but the activity seemed to help settle my thoughts.

As I shuffled past my front window, I spotted Mick in the park, sitting with an empty chair across from him, the checker board set up and waiting. I toyed with the idea of joining him for a game, but knew that temptation was only to distract me from the fact this case seemed to be going nowhere.

I paced, looking at all the angles again. Stacia was the only other person that seemed like she might be worth a discussion. Maybe that should be my next move.

All my pacing didn't lessen my frustration. Finally, I gave up for the day. About that time Anna texted me she wasn't coming over tonight but heading straight into the station to work out before her shift. I sent her back a makeshift emoji using punctuation marks. Then I made a simple dinner of macaroni and cheese and ate alone while watching a sitcom. That show wasn't very funny but the next one was good for a few chuckles. Then came two more that fell flat. Maybe it was me, or maybe the quality of TV these days wasn't what it used to be.

Either way, I turned in early, and surprised myself at how quickly I fell asleep.

The telephone played into my dream for the first several rings. Then I came up through the fog of sleep. The blood red letters of my clock told me it was a little after six in the morning. I clicked on the lamp beside my bed. The small cell phone on the nightstand restarted the stock ringtone. The name on the narrow screen read *Anna*.

A sharp pang of concern shot through my belly. I cut the ring tone short by flipping it open.

"Hello?" I asked, leaning forward and rubbing my eyes.

"Hey, it's me."

I cleared my throat. "What's up? Are you okay?"

"I'm fine," Anna said. "Romeo went on a natural DOA a couple hours ago."

She meant a natural death. When someone's death is unattended by medical professionals, a patrol officer—like Romeo McClaren, in this instance—was dispatched to investigate. Although the vast majority of the deaths were due to natural causes, usually old age, the officer's presence is a safety mechanism to ensure it wasn't something else, such as a homicide or suicide.

"I was busy with my own calls and some paperwork, so I didn't bother checking the details of his call on the computer," Anna said. "Otherwise, I would have recognized the name of the victim. Anyway, it caught my attention when I heard the detective check out on scene."

I sat upright, fully awake now. If a detective responded to the scene, that meant the officer or the medical examiner believed the situation deserved a closer look.

"Who was the detective?" I asked her.

"Dow," she answered.

"Shit," I muttered, and I knew what she was going to say next. I asked her the question anyway. "The DOA?"

"Lawrence Pines," Anna said. "The description in the call says it was a heart attack."

26

I pulled up in front of the Pines home just as Detective Dow was stepping out the front door.

Anna gave me the address before hanging up, saving me the time it would take to look it up for myself. I would have found it eventually, though it might have taken me some time. I knew that was how she rationalized sharing it with me — it wasn't confidential and the only impact of her telling me was to save me time.

I was glad because even ten minutes of searching online would have caused me to miss Dow.

She scowled at me as she approached my car. I got out to meet her.

"Why are you here?" she asked.

"I heard Lawrence Pines died."

"How'd you know that?"

"Police scanner," I lied.

Dow eyed me suspiciously. She couldn't know what was said on the air prior to when she was dispatched. It wouldn't be at all out of the norm for a victim's name to slip into traffic in any number of ways. Short of going back to review all of the radio traffic regarding this call, she wouldn't be able to disprove my claim.

"Is it natural?" I asked Dow, forging ahead.

She flipped her stenographer-sized notepad closed and tucked away her pen. "I'm not telling you anything."

"If it was a homicide," I asked, "is Rena a suspect?"

Dow narrowed her eyes at me. "Why do you ask that?"

"Murders usually involve someone close. She's the only one I know of that's close to him."

"Where'd you learn that little gem? *Dateline?*"

I spread my hands. "Why the hostility? We both want the same result, remember?"

"Oh, I remember," she snarled. "It still doesn't make us the same. I'm a commissioned police detective. You're a failed cop working for a sleazy defense attorney. We're nothing alike."

My jaw tightened. "You're right about that," I growled back at her. "I'm the guy who does his job without hurling insults."

Dow shrugged. "If hearing the truth sounds like an insult, then I guess that tells you something, doesn't it?"

I stared at her for a few moments. Her stony expression was unreadable. "At least tell me how you're classifying his death."

"I can't divulge that information at the current time," she recited. "Ongoing case."

"I thought we had an understanding," I said. "A

shared goal."

"My reasons for sharing any details with you were limited to my desire to help the victim in my embezzlement case, which I only had because it was tied to a missing person case. Since Mr. Pines is no longer with us, any reason for helping you is likewise gone."

"The victim was the business," I reminded her. "If Lawrence is gone, I assume Rena now owns Fresh Pines. Your case situation hasn't changed."

"Don't tell me my job."

"You still have an interest in finding Laura Shelton?"

Dow paused. Reluctantly, she gave a terse nod. "Of course, but you're not going to find her."

"What makes you say that?"

She tilted her head and smirked. "Come on. You, of all people, should know stories like hers don't have a happy ending. Do you really think she's tucked away in a motel somewhere, reading up on countries with no extradition? Or already sipping Mai Tais on a beach?"

"You don't?"

Dow sniffed. "We both know she's most likely in a hole in the ground somewhere. We'll find her when some hunter stumbles onto her shallow grave because his dog starts digging it up."

Her callous words rubbed me the wrong way. "Even if that's true, isn't it still your job to find her?"

"Of course, it is. Hopefully, I will." A tight, mirthless smile creased her mouth, never touching her eyes. "But you won't. So, giving you any more information doesn't really help my case."

"You never know."

"Please." She crossed her arms. "All I've ever seen or heard of where you're concerned is bad results."

"You said before my past didn't affect you."

"That was before you were affecting my present." She motioned toward my car. "Go home, Kopriva. Leave death investigations to the professionals."

We stood still and silent for a minute or so, staring at each other. In the interest of fairness, I'd initially intended on sharing with her what I'd learned so far, including my interviews with Harper, Abby Groves, or anyone else she may not have spoken to. If she was shutting off the faucet on her end, I'd do the same.

It became entirely clear she wasn't going to share anything further, or even move, until I left. Finally, I opened my car door, got inside, started the engine, and left.

A few blocks away, I spotted a drive-thru coffee stand and got in line. While I waited, I debated going back to the house. Once Dow was gone, I could go to the door. Who would be there? Rena, I realized. She'd have no desire to see me. That much had been obvious from the beginning. The shock of her father's death would only make it worse.

If she were somehow involved in that death…

I pulled up to the window of the coffee hut and ordered an Americano with three shots. By the time the barista had finished the simple drink and handed it over, I'd decided there was no profit in going back to the Pines house. I'd expected Dow to be more forthcoming and that had been my primary reason for going to the scene in the first place.

I sipped the hot coffee while I drove. Anna said the narrative of the call in the police computer system described Pines's death as likely being a heart attack. That seemed like something that would be hard to fake, but there were probably drugs that could induce one.

My car suddenly lurched and jumped as I hit an unseen pothole. Hot coffee splashed out of the drink opening and burned the back of my hand. I let out a curse and put the cup into the console holder, shaking my burned hand and blowing on the skin.

Potholes were the scourge of River City roadways. Every mayor promised to fix them and none of them did.

While I tried to cool my hand, I returned to the question of Rena as a suspect. Why would she kill her own father? After all, she'd been angry at Laura mostly on his behalf. Specifically, that his retirement was delayed by the embezzlement.

I mulled that over for several blocks. Another possibility took shape. If Rena was eager to take over the business and Laura's theft delayed it, that would be another, different explanation for Rena's anger.

I sighed. Unfortunately, I didn't know that Rena was angling to be in charge, much less if her desire was strong enough to motivate her to kill her own father. It seemed far-fetched, at least with what I knew. I was weaving fictional possibilities, but how much did they live in the real world?

Maybe he really did die of a heart attack. Or, given his affection for Laura and recent events, maybe it was more accurate to say he died of a broken heart. Either way, he was out of the picture now.

The picture remained a messy one.

27

I drove to Erik Shelton's house, hoping to catch him before he left for work. No one came to the door, despite my loud knocks. I kept at it for a while, just in case he was sleeping off getting drunk or had a late hockey game. Or both, I suppose.

There was no answer, and eventually I gave up and trudged back to my car.

"Hey!"

I turned around thinking for a moment it might be Erik after all. The voice came from next door. A round-faced man in a pair of flannel pajamas stood in the doorway, the screen door pushed open.

"Don't you process servers have to stick to certain hours?" he grumbled. "Some people are trying to sleep."

I glanced down at my watch. It was after eight already but I apologized anyway. "I'm not serving papers," I added. "I'm trying to help him with finding his wife."

The man's expression softened. "Laura?"

"Yes. Did you know her?"

"Of course. We're neighbors."

I didn't know the neighbors on either side of my house. In fact, Mick and his checkerboard represented the friendliest I'd been with anyone in the neighborhood. Maybe neighbors were different up here.

"Sorry," I said. "Dumb question." I took a few steps toward him. "What's your name?"

"Greg." He crossed his arms above his ample belly. "Who are you, exactly?"

"Stefan Kopriva. I'm an investigator, trying to find Laura Shelton."

Greg's mouth turned down in a dubious frown and he grunted. "Huh. Erik actually hired someone?"

I didn't bother clarifying my client. Instead, I asked, "Sounds like that surprises you."

"I didn't think he'd bother. Too much pride."

"Too proud to search for his missing wife?"

Greg shrugged. "Honestly, I didn't know she was missing until the cops came by to ask about her. I figured she finally just left him." He gave his head a short shake. "It'd be for the best. She was too good for him. Me and Mona both thought so."

"Mona's your wife?"

He nodded.

"Was she close with Laura at all?"

"No more than I was. We knew Erik to say hi to. We both had a few longer conversations with Laura. You know, those times you happen to be out in the front yard at the same time, getting the mail, or whatever?"

"Sure."

"Anyway, she was a sweet woman. Erik? He's full of crap, if you ask me."

"What made you think she'd left him?"

Greg chuffed. "Oh, I don't know," he said sarcastically. "Maybe the big blowout they had the night she left?"

I tilted my head. "They had a fight?" I already knew this but wanted to hear Greg's version.

"Oh, yeah," he said, his head bobbing demonstratively. "Went on for a good ten minutes. Lots of yelling."

"Back and forth, or…?"

"There was plenty of Erik bellowing at her," Greg said. "Laura showed some backbone. She gave as good as she got."

"Could you tell what they were arguing about?"

"No. Only a few choice curse words were distinct enough to make out."

"Did it sound physical?"

His eyes narrowed. "Of course not. We would have called the cops right away." His irritated expression faded slightly, and he shrugged. "Truth was, it went on long enough we were about to call them anyway. Then she left in her car."

I digested the information slowly. Erik's star continued to rise when it came to my suspicion meter. "Did she look like she was hurt?" I asked. "Physically, I mean?"

"I couldn't tell you. I was at my kitchen window. All I saw was her backing out of the driveway, and she was gone."

"Did Erik follow her?"

"Nope." He scoffed. "Can you imagine Mister Wonderful chasing after some woman like a puppy dog? It wouldn't look too cool."

"You really don't like him, do you?"

"What's to like?"

I shrugged. "No argument here. You said you didn't interact much as neighbors. It seems like a lot of dislike for that little bit of contact."

"Oh, I know Erik from way back," Greg said. "We went to high school together, I'm sad to say. Even back then, he was the same."

"How's that?"

"Popular," Greg said, "and full of shit."

28

I left my card with Greg, along with a request that his wife, Mona, call so I could interview her. I didn't expect she'd have any earth-shattering information, but that was the part and parcel of investigations. You never knew what piece of information someone might have. *They* might not even know its significance.

Finding those important bits and pieces usually meant wading through a lot of interviews that ultimately turned out to be pointless. The problem was, I had no way of knowing which were the pointless ones and which were crucial. So, I interviewed them all.

It was the price of admission.

At the same time, I'd done enough for the morning. My stomach was grumbling and a frustrated weariness had settled over me. It wasn't an uncommon frustration in case work. The problem wasn't finding out nothing; instead, it was finding out something after something that muddied the waters.

I drove another few blocks and shook my head

at my own thoughts.

No, that wasn't it.

Not exactly.

I was finding tidbits, sure. They tended to point toward an outcome I didn't want to be true. That Laura wasn't on the run. That she was in a shallow grave, just as Dow predicted.

You should know stories like hers don't have a happy ending.

Oh, yeah. I knew.

When I got home to my quiet house, I flipped open the case file and stared down at the photo of Laura Shelton. Then I looked at the one Erik had texted me. The light in her eyes in the second photo was all but gone.

I cursed and leaned back on the small couch, rubbing my eyes with the heels of my hands. I tried to shake the feeling Laura was somehow counting on me, but I couldn't. A sense of foreboding hung over me, along with a touch of anger, of resolve.

I'm going to find her.

One way or another, I was going to find Laura Shelton.

I let that resolution sink in throughout the rest of the day. I pored over the thin case file several times, making notes that went nowhere. A brief call from Mona, Greg's wife, netted no new information of value. A dozen fruitless searches on the Internet resulted in the same empty outcome.

Pacing my small house didn't help much.

I kept at it until I received a quick call from

Anna. While we spoke, I looked around and realized it was approaching evening. I was exhausted so, after we bade each other good night, I ate some cold leftovers and went to bed.

29

In the dark of the bedroom, my phone chirped. I glanced at the alarm clock. It was almost seven. When I picked up the phone, I saw the name on the small screen. Missy Jardin. I flipped open the phone and pressed it to my ear. "Hello?"

She was crying on the other end of the line. "They beat him up," she managed to say.

"Beat who up?" I asked.

"Err — Eri — Erik-k-k," she sobbed. "We're at the haw — hosp-p-pital."

"Which one?"

"Holy F-f-family."

"I'll be there in twenty minutes," I told her, and hung up.

The receptionist at the ER resisted telling me where Erik was until I lied and said he was my brother-in-law. Grudgingly, she directed me to his room on the far end of the treatment area. There was no door, only a drawn curtain. I stood at the curtain and asked, "Missy? It's Stef."

A moment later, the curtain parted. The tear-streaked face of Missy Jardin stared out at me. "Thanks for coming," she said, her voice hoarse from crying.

"No problem." I stepped inside. Erik lay on the bed, his eyes closed. His battered face had multiple bruises and his nose looked large and flatter than I remembered. His left eye was swollen shut and his bottom lip was split. His right arm was draped across his belly, held in place with a splint.

Missy moved to Erik's bedside and took his other hand in both of hers. Erik stirred and opened his eyes. When he saw me, he lifted his head. His upper lips curled to reveal bloodstained teeth.

"You," he rasped.

I held up my hands. "I had nothing to do with this."

Missy looked from me to Erik and back to me again. "What?"

Neither of us bothered to answer. Instead, I asked, "What happened?"

Erik just stared at me, closed his eyes, and let his head fall back against the pillow. He even turned his face to the side, in case I didn't get the message he didn't want to talk to me.

I met Missy's questioning gaze. "What happened?" I repeated.

"That man attacked him," Missy said, her voice quavering.

"What man?"

"That thug. The boyfriend."

I wondered for a moment if Erik's philandering had caught up to him. Had he messed around with the wrong woman and it came back to bite him? I turned up my hands to Missy. "What boyfriend are we talking about?"

"The daughter's," she said. "From Laura's work."

It dawned on me then, and I felt foolish for not immediately making the connection.

She meant Rena's boyfriend.

Tyler Driggs.

For a brief second, I kicked myself for not tailing Tyler instead of chasing information at my house. If I'd have followed him last night, I might have witnessed the assault. Then I shook off the thought. Second-guessing myself for decisions like that didn't help me at all now.

"You're sure it was Tyler?"

Erik grunted indistinctly.

Missy nodded. "He's sure," she said. "He'd met him before at some holiday function for the business last year."

"What happened?"

Once again, Erik said nothing. After a few seconds, Missy said, "He jumped Erik this morning when he was leaving for work."

"At his house?" I asked.

Missy nodded, wiping away a fresh tear with a shaking hand.

"Have the cops been here yet?"

"Come and gone," she said. "I called you right

after they left."

I returned my gaze to Erik, my mind whirring. Why would Tyler attack Erik if he or Rena were somehow responsible for Laura's disappearance? It didn't make sense. I decided to prod Erik for an answer. "Why'd he come after you, Erik? What did he want?"

Erik lay on the bed, silent.

I turned back to Missy. "What'd he say to the cops?"

Missy's confused expression had returned. Her eyes flicked from me to Erik and back again, a repeat of her earlier action. "I don't understand," she said. "Is there a problem between you and Erik?"

"He doesn't feel like talking, I guess. Do you know why Tyler assaulted him?"

She shook her head blankly. Then she looked over at Erik and patted his hand.

"He threatened me," Erik said, not looking my way.

From the looks of Erik, it looked like Tyler did more than simply threaten, but I kept that observation to myself. "Threatened you how?"

"He wanted the money back. That Laura stole."

"He thinks you have it?"

Erik shifted a shoulder in an almost imperceptible shrug, still not meeting my gaze. "He said they'd sue me."

That seemed odd to me. Tyler Driggs threatening him was on brand, but wouldn't his threats be about suing Erik *or* forcing him to return the money? Then again, Tyler was clearly the muscle and not the brains in that relationship. He could be freelancing to impress Rena, or maybe she sent him and he messed up the delivery of the threat.

"Did the cops arrest Tyler?" I asked.

"I don't know," Missy said, staring at Erik, her face etched in concern.

"Did they say they intended to arrest him?"

"I... don't remember." She turned toward me again. "Why would they do this to him?"

"I don't know," I said, not looking at her. "Erik?"

Erik didn't reply.

"What'd you and Laura argue about the night she left?" I asked him.

Erik shifted his head. His right eye opened to a slit. "What?" he asked gruffly, not moving his jaw when he spoke. "I told you already."

"Not all of it."

Next to him, Missy released his hand and sat back in her chair, folding her hands on her lap and watching us, her expression difficult to gauge.

"I said all I'm going to say." Erik glared at me with his one good eye. His gaze bounced between Missy and me.

"It might help me find her," I pressed.

"Fuck off," he growled.

"Okay." I turned to go and stopped. "Hey, who's Stacia?" I asked, remembering the timekeeper Oliver Santos had mentioned.

Erik didn't miss a beat. "I said... *Fuck. Off.*"

I spared a moment to meet Missy's confused eyes before I slipped through the curtain and left the emergency room. Obviously I wasn't going to get any answers here. To find out what I wanted to know, I'd have to go back to one of my least favorite places on earth.

30

At the police station, I forced myself to be patient —
never my strong suit — as the long line wended its
way toward the security station. Then I had to be
even more patient while explaining to a different
security guard why my prosthetic was setting off
the metal detector. This resulted in another
wanding. Once again, my irritation flared.

It was at times like this that snarky thoughts
about the security invaded my mind. He was just
some power head who didn't have what it took to
be a cop, so he spent his day hassling people at the
entrance to the Public Safety building.

I frowned and immediately chastised myself for
that thought. One of my few friends in the world,
Clell, was a security guard and he wasn't a power
head. He might be the nicest person I knew. As to
whether or not he had what it took to be a cop? Well,
I had no room to talk, given my own fall from grace.
Who says that skill set is entirely a good one?
Necessary, sure. Admirable? I was less certain of
that than I used to be.

When the guard finished screening me, he

waved me forward. I made directly for the police front desk. There wasn't an officer present, but a senior volunteer stood at the ready. He looked about seventy, but his eyes were sharp and discerning. I told him who I wanted to see and he nodded politely and made a call. After a few brief words, he hung up.

"Detective Dow will be out in a moment."

That surprised me. I'd expected her to be too busy or simply unwilling to talk to me. At best, I'd hoped she might have the senior volunteer hand the phone to me for a quick conversation. Instead, a couple of minutes later, she exited the secure area and walked over to meet me.

"Let's step outside," she suggested.

I didn't argue. We made our way out of the building and into a small courtyard between the Public Safety building and the Courthouse. In recent years, the city added a number of benches throughout the plaza. Dow chose the one furthest away from the door, with no one nearby.

"What's up?" she asked, a little guardedly. She held a pen in one hand and a steno notepad in the other, but made no move to flip it open.

"Erik Shelton got assaulted," I told her.

"I'm aware."

"He's saying it was Tyler Driggs who did it."

"I know that, too."

"Do you believe him?"

Dow shrugged. "I don't care to speculate. Besides, it's not my case."

"Not your…" I tilted my head. "You've still got the Laura Shelton case, right?"

"Yes."

"Then why wouldn't they assign this one to you?"

"That's above my pay grade. You'd have to ask Lieutenant Crawford."

I watched her for a few seconds. Then I said, "The two events are related."

"Maybe," she admitted. "We don't know for sure."

"Why would Tyler attack Erik?"

"You tell me," Dow said coolly. "You've been traipsing around, kicking at the ant pile. Why would he?"

"Kicking at the ant pile? I've been doing my job."

Dow pursed her lips and said nothing.

I took in a deep breath and let it out slowly. Irritation gnawed at the edges of my mind suggesting words that would be of little help here. "Let's try this — who has the assault case?"

"Detective Matsuda."

I resisted a frown. Detective Richie Matsuda. Great. Another cop who didn't like me. Matsuda's distaste went all the way back to my first foray into investigations. Along with the now-thankfully-retired Detective Jack Stone, he tried his damnedest to jam me up on specious charges involving the missing teenage girl I'd been hired to find. While the more troubling crimes they floated didn't stick, I still ended up spending a short time in jail on a plea arrangement. The likelihood of Matsuda returning a phone call for me was low to zero.

"Does Matsuda think it was Tyler Driggs?"

"He must," said Dow. "He got a felony assault warrant for him."

I stared at her. "Why couldn't you have just told me that to start with?"

She spread her hands. "Sorry. I'm still getting used to working with outside investigators. Playing things close to the vest is a habit."

I couldn't tell if she was being sincere or sarcastic, so I took her at face value. I noticed the cuff of my jeans had caught on my prosthetic. I reached down and snapped it into place. "I know the assault isn't your case, but I'd still like to hear your opinion. Why do you think Tyler went after Erik?"

"Maybe Erik tried fooling around with the daughter, Serena," Dow suggested.

"Why would he do that?"

She gave me a knowing look.

"Besides that," I said.

"Who knows?" Dow said. "He may have seen how vulnerable he is civilly. It's a community property state. He could have wanted to cozy up to her in order to stave off a lawsuit."

"If so, he failed," I told her. "Tyler supposedly threatened to sue while he was throwing Erik a beating."

Dow didn't appear surprised. "Doesn't mean Erik couldn't have tried something with the daughter, too."

I considered. From a human behavior standpoint, the scenario made sense. Erik had certainly shown that tendency. But I couldn't bring myself to buy it.

"You don't think so?" Dow asked.

"Rena doesn't seem like Erik's type," I said.

"His type seems to be any female with a pulse."

I turned over a hand and tilted my head from side to side. "Ehhh… that's fair. I don't think he's Rena's type, either."

"You got to know her that well?" Dow asked, light sarcasm riding under her words. "You work fast."

"It's not definitive," I said. Irritation burrowed into my chest, a low burning ember now. "Just a gut feeling."

"I wish I could do my job that way," Dow said, "instead of having to worry about probable cause."

I ignored the dig, though the ember flared up, like someone blowing on the coals of a dying campfire. "What if Tyler did it *for* Rena?"

"I think that's what I just said."

"No, not out of jealousy or whatever but to get information."

"Like what?"

"Information about the money."

"Erik didn't steal the money. His wife did."

"I know. Think about it. Whether she ran off with the money, or if Erik or someone else killed her, it still makes sense to think Erik might know something about the money."

She shrugged. "Okay, say that's the motive. So what?"

"It seems to put some more weight on the Erik-as-suspect side of the scale, doesn't it?"

Dow thought about it briefly. "Maybe," she admitted. "But Laura Shelton is still officially a missing person, possibly a fugitive."

"Do you have an arrest warrant for her yet?"

Dow hesitated then shook her head. "The missing person Locate is good enough for now. I'd rather find her and talk to her before getting the warrant."

I wasn't sure I understood that approach, but I wasn't going to question her professional decision-making. Instead, I said, "I talked to Greg."

"Greg who?"

"The next door neighbor."

"Ah. Okay."

I stared at her, waiting. When she didn't elaborate, I said, "He told me about the big fight Erik and Laura had, probably on the night she disappeared."

"Okay."

"You didn't mention that."

"It didn't seem relevant."

I gaped at her. "Not relevant? It paints a pretty clear picture of marital discord. The timing is important, too."

"Perhaps. It doesn't change the situation. Laura Shelton either ran away or was murdered. There is zero evidence of a murder—"

"That's what you think happened, though, isn't it?"

Dow closed her mouth and leaned back against the bench, appraising me. "What I think doesn't matter. What matters is what the evidence tells me. There is no evidence she was murdered."

"A huge fight with her husband doesn't count?"

"No. That's simply another fact, one that could just as easily point to her purposefully disappearing under her own power."

"For which there is also no evidence."

"Except that she's gone."

"It seems to me," I said, "that someone trying to hide is going to leave some sort of a footprint or an indicator."

Dow's gaze was cold. "You've found such evidence?"

"No, and neither have you, unless you're not sharing it."

Dow stared at me, not answering.

I sighed and shook my head. "My point is the absence of any such evidence speaks to the possibility she *didn't* run. That maybe she was murdered."

"You could use the same logic to argue the lack of evidence for a murder," she observed dryly.

"You could," I admitted. "But a murder is a single act. If someone commits that act and doesn't make any mistakes, it's mostly over. The chances of getting caught don't necessarily increase as time passes. If anything, they decrease. Hiding out, being on the run, that's an ongoing event. Every day, every hour, is another opportunity to make a mistake and be found." I shook my head. "That hasn't happened."

"Maybe she's just really good at hiding," Dow said. "Or we're both bad at our jobs. Either way, all we're doing here is spinning our wheels with what ifs."

I shrugged. She was right. But talking through a case sometimes made for seeing information through a new lens which could lead to a different approach. That approach might be what cracks the case open. I had Clell for the occasional discussion and my progress reports to Harrity often doubled as the same. Anna was another option, though I tried not to go to that well too often. She was smart, and helpful, but sharing too much with her ran the risk of putting her in a compromising position.

Even though Dow's attitude remained sour and she shot down every idea I presented, answered questions only reluctantly, and showed me little respect, I still felt a kernel of gratitude for the time she'd given me. She might be an unwilling participant, but she was there. I reconsidered my earlier decision to share my own interview results with her.

Then she flipped open her steno pad, clicked her pen, and all that gratitude fell away.

"I need something from you," she said. "I've been assigned to a murder case. You knew the victim, a transient named Amos Cline."

An image of the grizzled man sprang to my mind. He'd been a witness in a murder case Joel Harrity was defending. I spent weeks trying to find him. Once I finally did, I set him up at a motel Harrity contracts with for housing witnesses. This was around the time my long-absent mother came back into my life and threw my world into chaos, so I stepped away from everything else to deal with the mess she made. I later learned Amos Cline was murdered.

"That was a couple of years ago," I said.

"Then you remember."

"I do. Why are you investigating now?"

"We got a tip."

"What kind of tip?"

"The confidential kind," she said. "Now, I need to ask you a few questions about your interactions with Amos Cline."

I opened my mouth to answer and a thought occurred to me, so I closed it again. I looked Dow directly in the eye. She returned my stare, her expression implacable.

"I'm a witness?" I asked. "That's it?"

"I assume so."

"You assume?"

"I won't know anyone's actual role until I interview them. All I know for sure is Amos Cline was murdered."

"So, I could somehow be a suspect?"

She shrugged. "Should you be?"

I realized then why she'd given me the time on

the Shelton case. It was all a poorly executed attempt at creating some kind of social debt. *I helped you, now you help me.* Only, as I thought back to her responses, she didn't really help me much at all. The only new detail she shared was that Detective Matsuda was assigned the case and got an arrest warrant, something I could have learned from the senior volunteer at the front desk. It was public information, after all.

The best move in that moment would have been to swallow that ember of irritation, along with any injured pride, and do my duty to answer her questions. I didn't do anything wrong and something I told her might help catch a killer. I knew that was not just the smart play but the right one, too. I'd end up talking to her about it eventually, anyway. The only difference would be whether it was on this bench or in Harrity's conference room with the lawyer present.

Dow raised a brow expectantly.

I didn't answer right away. Instead, I tried to tamp down the growing frustration and anger inside me. Not just at her manipulative behavior today, but at her icy treatment earlier. Throw Richie Matsuda's contempt onto the pile, too, for that matter, along with all the reluctance I'd encountered from other witnesses on this case.

Most of all Dow's contemptuous words from just a few hours ago rang in my ears. How, in her eyes, we were nothing alike.

The detective shifted her pen closer to the

notepad. "So, when did you first meet Amos Cline?"

I rose slowly to a standing position and looked down at her. "I'll have to consult with my employer," I told her, "to see if the sleazy defense lawyer wants his failed cop to share privileged information with the police or not."

Dow's expression registered no surprise.

I turned and walked away.

31

After my meeting with Dow, I drove around aimlessly for a little while, listening to the radio and trying to both think and not think at the same time. It's not some fancy Zen trick, just an attempt to clear the mind clutter a little without losing track of the case I'm focused on.

While I drove, a classic Neil Young song warbled out of the car speakers. He sang about an old man and how his and the singer's life were a lot alike. The singer is a young man in the song—Young even drops his age as twenty-four. At twenty-four, I was still in the midst of what I thought would be a long and heroic police career. Within a year, I'd make the worst mistake imaginable. There's a small grave—more of a scar in the ground, really—up at Forest Lawn cemetery because of my failure. The stone commemorates a little girl who will be forever six-years-old.

Afterward, I left the job and spent a decade ruining what I saw as an unworthy life. I've spent the last six years trying to recover from that.

Trying to forgive myself.

Only I know I never will.

As the lyrics from the song on the radio bounced around in my head, I knew they weren't about Amy Dugger or my fatal mistake. They weren't about failure or redemption. But the music itself and the ache in Neil Young's voice *felt* like it was. Even if it wasn't about my life, it was still about loss and pain and regret.

That felt close enough.

I'd only been working the Laura Shelton case for a few days, but I could feel it slipping away from me. I could feel the specter of failure lurking in the shadows.

Again.

The fading note of the final chords of the song sounded like an agreement, until it was overshadowed by the opening guitar strums of an Eagles song.

I snapped off the radio and drove home.

My house felt more like a prison than a sanctuary. I took to pacing through the rooms once more, running facts and people through my mind. At one point, I stopped at the window and looked out at the park to see Mick Darabont shuffling towards his car, a checkerboard tucked under his arm. In his other hand, he held a book and a small box that held the checker pieces. Apparently, he was giving up early today.

For a moment, I wished my life were that simple.

Read a novel in the sun. Play a game if there were any takers. Then I felt guilty for being ungrateful. Compared to where it used to be, my life was in a good place. *I* was in a good place. I had steady work—a purpose. I had Anna who loved me even though she knew everything there was to know, including the ugly parts.

I was letting the frustration of spinning my wheels on this case push me towards a darker place.

Not very Zen.

I made some lunch and ate in silence, focusing now on the Laura Shelton case. It bothered me that I didn't know whether the woman was alive or dead. Having a clear idea on which might help direct my next move. Where to put my effort. If she were missing, the point would be finding her, first and foremost. If she were dead, finding her was still important, but the emphasis of my investigation would be on discovering who her killer was.

The embezzlement aspect and her being found out pointed toward her being on the run. To a lesser degree, so did the fact she left the house under her own power after the fight with Erik.

But.

I hesitated. There were so many buts.

A knock came at the back door. Two short raps. That meant Clell. I brought my lunch dishes into the kitchen and dumped them in the sink on my way to unlocking the door. Clell waved as I approached. The drooping sides of his mustache framed his honest smile.

"Working late or going in early?" I asked him.

"Just finished a double," the heavyset security guard said. "The other guy was a no-show, no-call."

I heard the hint of disdain in his voice for such irresponsible behavior, but the sentiment was tempered as if Clell didn't entirely want to pass judgment. I could imagine him suggesting all sorts of possible, sympathetic reasons the errant employee might not have shown up without so much as a word.

"Coffee?"

"You know it," Clell said. He shrugged off his light jacket and draped it over the back of his chair before he sat at the small kitchen table.

I went to the cupboard for the Maxwell House coffee. After a short volley of small talk, Clell asked me what was wrong. I had to smile at that.

"How can you tell?"

He shrugged. "Just can. Something's eating at you. It's a case, I hope, and not something personal."

Unfortunately, for me, many of the cases ended up being personal, but I understood what he meant. "The one I'm working on is frustrating," I said.

"Tell me."

So, I did. As I related everything I knew to this point, I finished loading the coffeemaker. Clell listened the way he often did—with silent, rapt attention. When the coffeemaker beeped, I poured us each a cup and returned to the table. Clell dipped his chin to say thank you without interrupting. I continued until I brought him up to my most recent conversation with Detective Dow.

After I finished, we sat quietly for a few seconds. I could see Clell mulling it over. I knew he'd have some questions and some thoughts on the case, so I waited patiently.

Finally, he asked, "Who do you think scratched up your car and left that note?"

"I don't know. For all I know, it could have been someone who didn't like my park job."

"You said you were between the lines, though."

"People can be assholes," I reminded him.

"I suppose. A note is one thing. Keying up a paint job is another level of angry."

"See my previous statement," I said.

"Okay, but, *if* it was a warning, where might it have come from?"

"Unsure."

"Kinda makes for an ineffective warning, then, doesn't it?"

"I suppose it does."

"Could it have been the husband?"

"Erik? Why would he want me to stop looking?"

Clell lowered his glasses slightly and stared knowingly down his nose at me.

"So, you think he killed her?" I asked.

"I think you think maybe he did."

I considered. It was a plausible scenario and, unfortunately, not an uncommon one. Anna's true crime reality shows were a testament to that.

"Of course," Clell continued, "from what you told me about the daughter's boyfriend, this Tyler guy, angry seems to be right up his alley."

I nodded. Tyler would be a more likely candidate, behavior-wise. What still bothered me was, "Why key my car? There's no reason for him to want me to stop investigating."

"Unless it's the same reason Erik might have, if either he or the daughter are responsible for Laura's death."

I frowned. "I mean, it could be, I suppose. What's the motive? The stolen money? Frustration over the lackluster police response?"

"I don't know," Clell admitted. "I'm just talking possibilities." He thought for a second. "It certainly wasn't the old man."

For a second, my mind flashed back to the Neil Young song on the radio from earlier. Then I realized he meant Lawrence Pines. "That's not true," I said. "If someone killed Laura, it could have been Pines. Just because he's dead now, doesn't mean he couldn't have done the deed earlier."

"The way you told it, it didn't sound like you thought he had it in him," said Clell. "He considered her like a daughter."

"Maybe that was his motivation. Betrayal. Revenge."

"Sure, if he's the kind of person who thinks money is worth someone's life."

"There are plenty of people in the world who think like that."

"Plus, you said he was religious."

"Religion has resulted in more killing than just

about anything else," I said, the cynicism in my voice apparent even to my own ear.

"Sad, but true," Clell agreed. "That stood out to me when you explained it. Everyone seems to be wearing a mask of some kind."

"Masks, huh? Like who?"

"Take your pick. The husband, Erik, wants people to think he's worried about his wife, but that's a mask. He seems more concerned with playing hockey and cheating on her."

I turned over my hands in agreement. Clell had a point.

"It's true of all the rest, too. The business owner may be gone now, but he wanted everyone to think he cared more about Laura than the money. It seems, when you delved a little deeper, it wasn't that he was disappointed — he was angry about the cost of the audit and frustrated the police didn't seem to do anything while Laura ran. In the end, it *was* about the money."

"Of course, it was. He owned a business. It's all about the money."

"That wasn't the mask he showed you initially."

I thought back to my first meeting with Lawrence Pines. "No, it wasn't. Not entirely."

Clell nodded. "The daughter put on a mask of being concerned about her father's retirement but, if that's the case, why'd she send her boyfriend to beat up Erik? To find the money somehow?"

"That's my theory, at least at the moment."

"Why now?" Clell asked. "Her father was

already dead. If she truly cared about his retirement, she would have sicced Tyler on Erik a day or two after Laura disappeared. Instead, she waited until her father was gone. That tells you her concern was about the money itself, not her father's retirement, like she said."

"Maybe it was just revenge that took a little longer," I suggested.

Clell looked at me while he thought it over. Then he shook his head. "It seems too unfocused for revenge. Unless she thought Erik was in cahoots with Laura."

"Cahoots?" I said. "Nice word, grandpa."

Clell's eyes narrowed. "It's a perfectly good word."

I held up my hands in surrender. "Any other masks you want to tell me about?"

"The detective," Clell answered. "She tried to put one on, as a collaborator, to butter you up to answer her questions about Amos Cline."

"True enough."

"Lots of masks," he said. "None of them doing a very good job of hiding much, seems to me. Everyone's disguise has quickly grown thin. Not entirely see-through, but… thin."

I thought about what he said and realized I was nodding slowly in agreement. "Even Laura," I murmured.

"I hadn't thought of that," Clell said. "I suppose it's true. I mean, I get that she was stealing from her employer. That's a mask, for sure."

"That's not what I meant," I told him. I rose and went to retrieve the case file. Then I showed Clell the picture of Laura inside it and the one Erik had texted to me on my phone. I stood and watched him as his compassionate eyes shifted from one to the other.

"It's like two different people," he said quietly.

I noticed his coffee was gone. Mine was nearly there, too, so I grabbed both to refill them. "How do you mean?"

Clell didn't answer right away. When I plunked down a full cup of coffee near him, he didn't reach for it. Instead, he tapped the table next to the photo of a smiling Laura in a bridesmaid dress. "There's a bloom on her here in this one," he said.

I leaned forward. "A bloom?" I had an inkling of what he meant, but I wanted to be sure.

He lifted one shoulder in an apologetic half-shrug. "I heard it in a movie once. It made sense to me. It's like there's a light inside her, a special something. It's pure. Happy." He looked up. "It makes people want to be around a person."

I looked down at Laura's photo again. Clell was right. There *was* a bloom to her. Something joyous and compelling. It's what I'd noticed before but didn't have a name for it. The idea someone might have snuffed out that light burned in my gut.

"In the one on your phone…" Clell said, then paused. "I mean, maybe it's because it's so small on your tiny screen, but it looks like all the joy has been trampled out of her."

"Maybe it was just a bad day," I offered, though I didn't entirely believe my own words. "Or maybe she's normally a sad person and the other photo was one good day."

"Is that what people are telling you?"

I thought of Ted the barber, Abby Groves, and Greg the neighbor, not to mention Missy Jardin. "No," I admitted. "But someone wouldn't steal all that money if she were happy. If she had any remorse in her soul, the continued theft would make her unhappy, wouldn't it?"

"It would," Clell said quietly.

"Maybe that was it. All the weight of her actions coming to bear."

Clell shook his head emphatically. "No, this is something deeper. Like the entire foundation of her life has been shattered." He looked up at me. "Something bad happened to this woman."

His words echoed loudly in the air. I was afraid they were true. Afraid Laura Shelton's tragic downfall didn't stop with depression or sadness, but ended in an unmarked grave somewhere yet to be discovered. I was also amazed at Clell's insight.

"You got all that from a photo?" I asked, impressed.

Clell glanced down into his cup, suddenly bashful. "Working security gives me a lot of time to watch people," he said, "and to think."

"Time well spent," I mused.

He shrugged. "I don't know if it helps or not. I could be wrong."

I glanced down at Laura's smiling face as she came through the doorway in her bridesmaid dress. "No," I said. "You're definitely not wrong."

Clell leaned back and yawned. "I better head home and get some shut-eye. Next shift will be starting before I know it."

I thanked him for listening to me and offering his help.

"I hope you find her," Clell said, at the door. "And not..." He trailed off, as if he didn't want to speak her fate aloud once more.

"Me, too," I told him.

After Clell left, I mulled over my next move while making scrambled eggs.

Every case was different, I'd learned, but in some ways, they were also all the same. When it seems like you're making zero progress, all you can do is keep moving forward. Keep tugging at the strings until you find one that unravels the sweater.

Hailey might be one such string. Erik had a fling with her, after all. And her Aunt Viola might have been naturally protective of her, but perhaps there was something more there. Either way, I'd need to contact her somewhere other than the bar if I expected to have any chance at a productive interview.

So, I decided the next string would be Stacia, the timekeeper from the hockey rink. Talking to her — if she'd even talk to me — probably wouldn't be any more helpful than my trip to the Swinging Doors had been. Yet, it was a string I could pull. You never knew.

My notes said there was an over-fifty game starting in less than an hour. I finished up my eggs, rinsed my plate and headed out.

In the car, I left the radio off.

About halfway up to the hockey rink, my phone chirped. When I glanced down, the number looked familiar, but I couldn't place it.

"Hello?" I asked, pressing the phone to my ear.

"Hi," the female voice said. "It's Abby. Abby Groves?"

"I remember," I said, picturing the dog-training flyer and her pleasant features. "What can I do for you, Abby?"

"I need to talk to you."

"All right. Go ahead."

"No. In person. Can you meet me at the same place as before?"

"Coffee Tawk?"

"That's it."

"When?"

"Is now possible? I have a break in my schedule, and—"

"I'll be there in twenty minutes."

<h1 style="text-align:center">32</h1>

I actually made the drive in closer to fifteen minutes. When I walked into the spacious coffee establishment and looked around, I immediately spotted Abby in the same seat we'd occupied before. I walked over and sat across from her.

"Thanks for coming," she said.

"Thanks for calling," I replied, cautiously hopeful. "What can I do for you?"

Abby shifted uncomfortably in her seat, glancing away. When her gaze returned to me, her expression was troubled.

"You seem torn about something," I prodded gently.

Abby nodded slowly. "A little. I guess I've made my decision, or I wouldn't have called you."

I waited.

After a few seconds, she continued. "I lied to you before." She took a deep breath and let it out. "I mean, I told myself I was doing it out of loyalty to Laura because, if she's managed to get out of this situation and is living happy somewhere, I didn't want to ruin that. If she didn't want to be found, I shouldn't—"

"Where is she, Abby?" I asked, keeping my voice even.

Abby stopped. Slight confusion crossed her face. "I don't know. I suppose, in a way, that's why I called you."

"What do you mean?"

"You said something during our conversation that stuck with me. That something bad could have happened to Laura." She paused and wet her lips before continuing. When she spoke, her voice quavered with emotion. "I never considered that. I assumed she ran off with the money and I was, like, *good for her*, you know? That business never valued her highly enough and her husband was a shit, so… well, that was how I wanted to think of her."

"What is it you want to tell me?"

"I'm only telling you because if he did something to hurt Laura, or if Erik found out and that's what caused him to—"

"Abby, what is it?"

Abby took another long, wavering breath. "Erik wasn't the only one having an affair," she said. "So was Laura."

I sat back slightly, surprised. "She was?"

Abby nodded. "At first, I think it was revenge, to get back at Erik for cheating on her. Despite all that gaslighting, she knew he had, so she figured turnabout was fair play. She planned on telling him about it, rubbing his face in it so he could see how it felt. But she said things quickly turned into something else. Not necessarily love, but something nice. So, she kept it a secret."

"Who was she seeing?" I asked.

Abby swallowed, then told me.

"It was Ted. The barber who worked next door."

33

Ted had someone in the chair when I arrived. He glanced up at the sound of the bell above the door dinging, flashed me a welcoming smile, and turned back to the head of hair he was working on. I took one of the seats lining the opposite wall to wait. The hard steel of my Kahr .40 pressed against the small of my back while I waited for Ted to finish up with the sole customer.

Bringing the gun felt like overkill but I decided to follow the oldest gun lover's adage: better to have it and not need it, as it were. Ted may have seemed like a decent, mild-mannered guy but I wasn't taking any chances.

The shop was eerily quiet except for the light strains of the oldies station coming from the back of the room and the snip of Ted's scissors. He and the customer didn't speak while Ted worked. I could appreciate that he knew when the customer didn't want to talk. I'd had some experiences that felt more like interrogations than haircuts.

Say one thing about Ted—he was efficient. In less than five minutes, he'd finished, cleaned off the customer and taken his money. After a cordial farewell, the doorbell dinged again — to signal departure this time — leaving the two of us alone. I took the opportunity to stand up, just in case the coming moments went poorly.

Ted motioned toward the empty chair.

I shook my head. "Not here for a trim."

"Oh." Ted's hands dropped to his sides. His expression drifted toward wariness. "Still looking for Laura?" he asked. "Any luck?"

In that moment, something happened in the undercurrent of the energy between us. I knew for certain Abby Groves had been telling the truth. I could sense it in Ted's voice, his expression, his body language. What's more, it was clear he knew I knew about him and Laura. All of the societal niceties and pretenses remained in place, of course, but the veil had been pulled back, and we both knew it.

Any transcript of our brief conversation so far would show none of that. My realization — and his — wasn't something Harrity or any other lawyer could use in court. But it was just as real to me as any hard evidence, and I've learned to trust these realizations when they happened.

Since it was just the two of us alone in that room, I took the direct approach.

"How long have the two of you been seeing each other?" I asked him. I kept my tone non-accusatory, but left no doubt as to the facts.

No surprise showed in Ted's eyes. He opened

his mouth slightly, as if to protest then closed it again. Nervously, he wiped his hands on his barber's smock. I was keenly aware of the needle-tipped scissors he'd slid into one of the pockets there.

"How'd you find out?" he asked, sounding defeated.

"Does it matter?"

He shrugged. "We promised not to tell anyone."

"Secrets never keep," I said. "Not as long as someone alive is holding onto them."

Ted winced slightly at my words. He wiped his hands again and swallowed. "It's just… we thought if we kept it a secret, it wouldn't have to end."

I watched him carefully. "Is that what happened, Ted? Did someone find out?"

"Someone must have. You're here." He reached for a small broom and set about expertly sweeping up the detritus from his last customer. "No one was supposed to know," he muttered.

"Where is she now, Ted?"

Ted's eyes cut to mine. "I don't know."

"Then tell me what happened."

He lifted the small dustpan full of hair and dumped it into a nearby garbage can. Then he replaced the broom and dustpan along the wall. He cast a longing glance toward the front door, as if hoping for an interruption that would rescue him from this conversation.

"Ted?"

He turned back to me. "We were friends," he

said. "I already told you that. We took our smoke breaks together."

"That led to an affair?"

"It wasn't like that."

"What was it like, then?"

Ted took a deep breath and let it whoosh out. "We talked. I mean, we *really* talked, not like the meaningless chatter that goes on in here most days. I listened to her, she listened to me. Like I said, we were friends."

"And then?"

"And then..." He heaved another sigh. "Then she found out her piece of garbage husband was fooling around. Even though he denied it to the ends of the Earth, she knew. She'd suspected for a while, but knowing for certain was hard to take, especially coming on the heels of getting frozen out on all the partner talk with her boss. It was a double shot of bad news."

"And, so...?"

His tongue darted out to lick his lips. "So, we talked about it. She said she wanted to get even with Erik. She asked me to help."

"Let's be clear," I said. "She asked you to sleep with her for revenge?"

Ted nodded.

"And you did, I take it?"

He nodded again. "She was my friend."

"A friend with benefits," I mused.

"It wasn't like that."

"Yeah, you said that a few seconds ago. Ted,

that's exactly what it sounds like."

"Maybe," Ted allowed. "However we started, it became something more."

"For how long?"

"Over two years now."

I raised a brow. "All this time, no one knew?"

"No one," he agreed, "except for whoever told you."

It was an implied question. Ted was fishing for my source. I ignored the attempt and moved on. "Once is revenge. Two years is… a relationship."

"It was." He paused, and added, "It was the best relationship of my life."

Was. The word clanged in my mind. I knew he could be using it because the relationship was over. But another possibility whispered its horrible potential in my ear.

"So, not casual," I said, keeping my voice even.

"Not for me. I was in love with her."

"Did she feel the same?"

Ted stared back at me, not answering. His silent, pleading expression was answer enough.

I shifted my stance subtly, so my body was slightly more bladed toward Ted. My mind continued to whir with possibilities. Did Laura try to break off the relationship? Did Erik find out? Did Ted know about the money? Or, worst of all, did he have something to do with her disappearance?

"What happened, Ted?" I asked again, keeping the question open-ended.

He spread his hands. "I treated her right," he

said. "I listened. She really appreciated that. Lord knows, she wasn't getting that at home, or at work. Did she love me?" He dropped his hands to his side again. The scissors jumped and shifted in his pocket. "I don't know. I think so, in a way. She wasn't *in love* with me. She wasn't going to leave Erik for me."

"Did you two talk about that? Her leaving Erik?"

"A little. Once she made it clear it wasn't going to happen, it became something of a forbidden subject. Not worth talking about, since nothing was going to change."

"Did she say why she stayed married? Or why she kept working for the Pines?"

"Not exactly."

"How about *un*exactly?"

Ted shifted uncomfortably, glancing away again. "One time, when we were at…" He paused, shaking his head. "It doesn't matter where. We'd slipped away for a few hours. It was late spring and we were lying there with the window open. I had the radio playing and that song about life being a highway came on. You know the one? I think it's a Springsteen song."

"Tom Cochrane," I said immediately.

"You sure?"

I nodded. "I'm positive." The song was popular while I was at the police academy. Some guy from central Washington—was it Sunnyvale? I couldn't remember where. In fact, I struggled to recall the guy's name in that moment. Either way, he decided it would be our class anthem. The tune was catchy and others accepted the idea, so it was adopted. As a result, I must have heard it a hundred times during physical training, in the locker room, during lunch. It even made an appearance at our graduation ceremony.

Ted shrugged. "Either way, we were still at a point where she hadn't shut down the subject of me and her making a go of it." He waved dismissively at the shop we stood inside. "I'd sell out and head out, I said. With her. So I kinda joked about it. You know, like, 'See? Life is a highway, let's go ride it.' Then she didn't answer for a while. Finally, she said she was old enough to realize she'd passed most of the exits off the particular highway she was on. That, now, all that was left was to try to find some small joys along the way."

"Was that what she was doing with you?"

"I sure took it that way," Ted said. "Even though I told her she was being a pessimist. That made her chuckle. She called me naive, and said there was no sense trying to reorder a life already lived."

"As in, you've made your choices, now live with them?"

"I guess. My point to her was we're in our forties, not our eighties." A small, wistful smile crept onto his lips. "Plenty of highway left."

"How'd she respond to that?"

"She didn't. That was the end of the conversation, and any others on the topic." His voice tightened and he glanced away, clearing his throat. "I would have gone with her," he croaked. "I always told her I would. I just wanted to be with her. We'd be fine. I can cut hair anywhere. We could go… anywhere."

"She didn't like that idea?"

"Apparently not," he said, mournfully. "She left without me."

"Left without you?" I repeated, watching him carefully.

He lifted his hands again in a futile gesture. "I was hoping you'd find her and maybe I'd get another chance to talk to her about… us." He peered more closely at me. "You haven't, have you? Found her, I mean?"

"No, not yet."

Ted seemed to deflate. He collapsed into the nearby barber chair. "Maybe she's really gone for good, then."

"For good?"

He nodded dumbly. "I wish I knew where. I wish…" He trailed off, staring into space.

"What if she's dead?" I asked quietly.

Ted's eyes snapped to mine, anger flashing in them. "Don't say that!"

"It's a possibility."

"No," he growled. "She's not… she's not *that*. I'd know. I'd feel it." He tapped his chest meaningfully.

I thought of all the parents out there with missing kids who expressed similar sentiments for years, only to eventually discover the unpalatable truth. Like Ted, they didn't *know*. They only *felt* what they wanted to feel, what they wanted to believe. Maybe what they needed to believe. Regardless, it didn't change the objective truth.

I wondered if it were the same truth when it came to Laura Shelton.

"Ted," I said, "you need to tell me what happened."

His hard stare softened with confusion. "I did."

"I mean a couple weeks ago, right before she left. Was there an argument? Did she refuse to take you with her? If things got out of hand, it's understandable but you need to tell me."

Ted's confusion slipped into disbelief. "You think *I* hurt her?"

"Did you?"

"God, no!" Ted shook his head emphatically. "I told you, I loved her. Why would I…?"

"In my experience, people do all kinds of things because of love. Not all of them are positive. Sometimes they regret those things afterward."

He gaped at me. "Regret? The only regret I have was she didn't want to leave with me. That she didn't love me enough to…" His voice caught and he looked away. When he turned back to me, his eyes glistened with tears. They also burned with anger. "I don't know where she is," he said, his words coming at me like daggers. "When I think of her now, I hope she's somewhere safe and she's happy. Even if I knew where that was, there's no way I'd tell *you*. Especially not now."

"Ted…"

The barber sprang to his feet and leveled a finger

at me. "Get out of my shop. Now."

I paused a moment, considering whether or not to push him some more.

Ted's hand curled into a fist. "I mean it," he said, his voice low. "I haven't been in a fight since the fifth grade but, so help me, if you don't leave in the next three seconds, I am going to beat the shit out of you."

I held up my hands to calm him and slowly slid backwards until I reached the door. Then, I turned and left.

34

Outside, I started down the sidewalk to where I'd parked.

Ted's anger was interesting. If he was a spurned lover who turned on the object of his affections, the anger made sense. But I didn't get the feeling anger was part of Ted's usual makeup. He struck me as far more affable. It was likely that specific was the trait that resulted in his relationship with Laura. If he'd been an angry person by nature, the friendship that led to an affair was unlikely to have happened.

Extreme actions—like killing someone—are often driven by extreme emotions. By his own admission, Ted loved Laura. Love can motivate people to act well outside their usual comfort zone—both positively and negatively.

Like murder.

I shook my head while I walked. Could Ted have killed Laura over being rejected? Maybe. Anything was possible. But it sounded like he'd already accepted his role in her life. He might find it heartbreaking, he might wish for more but, to my ear, he'd resigned himself to his fate. Explosive situations like being rejected and then murdering your lover don't usually result from such acceptance or resignation. They come more from having a belief or expectation that gets shattered in a moment, sometimes causing a tectonic shift in a person's entire life or world view. It's the whiplash input that causes the snap decision output.

That wasn't Ted.

I believed he'd been angry enough he would have thrown hands at me if I'd stayed. However, that reaction was in defense of the idea of what he and Laura had shared. My suggestion he could have hurt her fit the whiplash moment and caused his emotional response. Outside of these dynamics, I doubted Ted was angry or prone to violence enough to have hurt Laura.

I stopped suddenly, about twenty feet from my car.

Angry.

Violent.

I knew someone who was both.

I turned around and headed back up the street.

The buzzing sound when I opened the front door to Fresh Pines announced my arrival. The employee who'd been at the counter the last time I'd visited was gone. I waited, and a few seconds later Rena Pines walked out of the back holding a file in her hands. When she recognized me, her lip curled.

"What do *you* want?"

"I came to talk to Tyler."

She snorted. "The cops have already come by. He's not here."

"Then you know he has a warrant?"

"I know there's some bullshit going on." Her eyes narrowed. "Wait, did *you* have something to do with that?"

"No."

"You probably did." She shook her head. "What do you want? I'm busy."

"I imagine so."

"What's *that* supposed to mean?"

"Easy." I held up my hands. "Don't get angry. All I meant was there must be a lot to attend to with your father's passing and all."

Her suspicion didn't diminish. "That's dumb to say. Of course, there is."

"Did you know about Laura wanting to be a partner in the business?" I asked.

"I'm not talking about private affairs with you."

"It's all starting to make sense," I said.

"What is?"

"You're an angry person. You're with an angry, violent person. Laura was a threat."

Rena let out a bark of derisive laughter. "Ha! You're an idiot."

"Your father said she was like a daughter to him and —"

"Shut up about my father!" Rena raged, pointing a finger at me. "You have no right to talk about him."

"Laura was taking your place, wasn't she?" I prodded. "Replacing your role in the business and as a daughter."

Rena flung aside the file and stomped toward me. "You little, fucking bug! How dare you!"

I shuffled backward. My hand drifted toward the small of my back. If Tyler were lying low here at Fresh Pines, he'd be coming out of hiding any moment. Failing that, Rena herself looked like she could be a handful.

"This can't be the first time someone has suggested this to you," I said. "I'm sure the cops made it clear you were a suspect."

Rena stopped short of coming around the counter. Her fists were balled and her nostrils flared. Then she said, "I wish Tyler were here, you little puke. He'd kick your ass and make you eat those words."

"Eat the truth?"

"You don't know shit."

"Where's Laura, Rena? Where'd you bury her?'

Rena leaned back her head and laughed sharply. There was no humor in the sound. Then she fixed me with a dark look. "You're about as clueless as they come, aren't you? Was this your plan? You'd come in here and make your little accusation and I'd confess? *Oh, yes, I killed Laura and buried her in the woods. Here's a map.*" She held out her empty hands, miming the act. "X marks the spot." Then she lifted her middle finger to me. "You're a fucking idiot."

"The truth will come out, eventually," I told her.

"It always does."

"I hope so. Then you'll see what a moron you are." She dropped her vulgar gesture. "I didn't touch a hair on that bitch's holier-than-thou head. Dad may not have seen her for what she was but I did. She was a thief and a liar. Even without knowing that he still wasn't ever going to give her a piece of my birthright. As far as replacing me as his daughter, if you think that, you're even stupider than you already look."

I watched her while she ran through all of her denials. What she didn't realize is she'd just outlined her motivations for murdering Laura in exacting detail. *Methinks thou doth protest too much,* and all that.

"You might think I'm stupid," I said evenly, "but even if I am, the cops are on this case. Everything will come out eventually. It'll be better for you if it is sooner, while it can still look like the heat of the moment. A crime of passion."

Rena clenched her jaw. "I don't think you're stupid. You *are* stupid. You're looking in all the wrong places."

"Where else should I be looking?"

"Not here," Rena snapped. "But I don't give a shit. Even if you find her, my money is gone."

"Maybe she stashed it away somewhere."

"Sure," she said, sarcastically. "And maybe I have a fairy godmother who will tell me where it is." Rena shook her head. "The money's gone. She'll never be able to pay it back. So I've got nothing more to say to you."

She pointed emphatically past me.

"Go."

There was no use trying to continue the conversation. For the second time that morning, I backed my way to the door, and left.

In my car, I withdrew my gun from the small of my back and replaced it in the glove box. Then I checked the time, wondering if there was still a chance to catch Stacia the timekeeper at the rink.

35

I wasn't sure how long recreational league hockey games lasted. Professional hockey games went for two-and-a-half to three hours, but I doubted rec games took as much time.

I drove up to the rink, anyway. When I arrived, the scoreboard told the story — there was less than five minutes remaining in the third period. A dark haired woman sat in the scorekeeper's box next to the rink.

I decided to get a hot chocolate and wait. The snack bar was staffed by a woman considerably younger than the suspicious employee I'd spoken with before. As I paid her for the small drink, I asked, "Is that Stacia running the clock?"

"Sure is." She handed me my change.

I thanked her and took a seat in the lobby. Sipping my hot cocoa, I watched the final few minutes of the game play out. After the buzzer sounded, Stacia waited for the players and referees to exit the ice. Then she reset the scoreboard to eighteen minutes and zeros on each side. Finally, I watched her leave the scorer's table and walk toward the lobby.

Stacia looked to be in her late twenties. She wore tight jeans, gray boots, and a stylish, oversized white sweater. Her dark hair hung past her shoulders and was teased up a bit. I had the impression that 1980s fashion might be making a comeback.

She stopped briefly at the snack bar where the attendant already had a coffee ready for her. I stood and approached.

"Stacia?" I asked.

She glanced up, no recognition in her face as she struggled to place me.

"My name's Stefan Kopriva," I said. "I'm an investigator. Can I talk to you for a minute?"

Confusion creased her features. "An investigator?"

I motioned toward the empty seats in the lobby area. After a moment, Stacia gave a little shrug and walked toward them. She sat down and crossed a leg over her knee. Her foot bounced nervously as she sipped her coffee.

"What's this about?" she asked. "I didn't do anything wrong."

"I know," I said, though the truth was, I didn't know anything about her. "I'm talking to you for background information. As a witness, essentially."

"A witness to what?"

"I'm looking for a missing woman," I said. "Laura Shelton."

It took a moment for the name to sink in. Then

Stacia's expression turned sour. "I don't know anything about her."

"You knew her husband, though, right?"

"Yeah," she admitted. "The lowlife prick." Her index finger uncurled from the Styrofoam cup she held and she pointed it at me. "I didn't know he was married, okay? If I did, I never would've taken up with him."

"I believe you."

"Good." Her eyes narrowed. "What does this have to do with his wife? Is she leaving him? Because, if so, good on her. That's why I called her."

My eyebrow lifted. "You called Laura?"

She nodded. "Someone had to tell her what a cheating bastard her husband is."

She already knew, I thought. Stacia's call wasn't the first time she'd received a call like that.

"What did Laura say?" I asked.

"Nothing. I got her voicemail, so I left a message. That was it." Stacia's expression remained sour. "I wish I'd found out what a man-whore he was before we hooked up."

"How long did the two of you see each other?" I asked.

Stacia tilted her head in thought. "Maybe three weeks or so."

"When did you find out he was married?"

"A couple of days after I broke it off with him."

It was my turn to tilt my head and look at her askance. "You broke up with him *before* you found out he was married?"

She nodded. "I was supposed to pick him up at his house one day after I finished up with the over-fifty games. We were planning on spending the day up at his lake cabin." She motioned toward the ice, where the Zamboni was making long passes to clean the ice surface. "Anyway," Stacia said, "the Zam broke down right in the middle of a scrape, so the game ended up being canceled. I headed over to Erik's a couple hours early and, when I pulled onto his street, I saw him standing in his doorway kissing another woman."

I winced sympathetically. "Ouch."

"Yeah," she agreed. "Not good." She took a steadying breath and looked down at her cup for a moment. "I should have been furious. I was, later. At the time, I just went cold."

"You didn't know," I said in consolation.

"I should have figured it. I mean, I knew he was a player, and, I mean, like, whatever, fine. Bang away. Just don't tell someone you're exclusive and then be a cheater. That's a whole other level. Then to find out later he was married the whole time?" She shook her head in disgust. "It makes him lower than whale shit in my book."

"Did you just drive away, or...?"

"Hell, no! I wanted to see what the son of a bitch would say. So, I pulled into the driveway as soon as she left and he went inside. I asked him who just left. Only, I left out how I saw him making out with her on his own porch. Instead, I said I'd only seen the car, not the person in it."

"He believed you?"

"Of course. He thinks he's so sly but he's not as smart as he thinks." Stacia shook her head again and paused to take a sip of her coffee. "Bastard told me the truth about who she was though. As soon as he said it, I realized he wasn't just a man whore, he was sewage."

"Who was it?"

Stacia raised her brow and met my eye. "It was Misty," she said.

"Misty who?"

"You, know, *Misty*." When I didn't react, Stacia said. "Come on, keep up. Misty? His sister-in-law?"

I sat back in my chair, stunned. "Missy, you mean?" I asked Stacia.

She waved her hand dismissively. "Misty, Missy, whatever. Point is, not only was this piece of trash cheating on me *and* cheating on his wife — who I never knew existed until after — he was doing it to both of us with his own sister-in-law." She stared at me for a long moment. "See? Bottom of the ocean, this guy. I'm talking Mariana Trench here."

I nodded slowly in agreement, the revelation still sinking in.

"So, if that's all…" Stacia said, starting to stand.

"Wait," I said. "I have a couple other questions."

Stacia frowned and sank back into her chair. "Reliving this isn't exactly fun, you know?"

"I'm sorry. I'll be quick."

She waved for me to continue.

"He told you it was Missy, his sister-in-law?"

"Uh, *yeah.*"

"So, that's when you figured out he was married?"

"That was my first reaction," Stacia said. "When

I asked, 'You're married?', he just laughed and said no, she was his brother's wife."

"He has a brother?"

"No!" Her frown deepened. "Such a liar."

Quick on his feet, too, I noted. I imagined him making the first excuse and realizing his mistake. His fictional brother was a slick recovery. It wouldn't hold up long term but I got the sense that, in Erik's mind, none of these dalliances were intended to last.

"Was it really Missy?" I wondered aloud. Then I met Stacia's eye. "He might have just used her name to cover for himself. That woman could have been anyone."

"I realize that," Stacia said, a little testily. "At the time, I didn't care. I caught him kissing another woman, and he lied about it. If it was actually his sister-in-law, that was even worse, but the kissing and the lying were already enough for me to dump his ass."

"So how do you know…"

"Have you ever been to Kitty's Koffee Korner?" Stacia interrupted.

I paused, all of the pieces falling into place. "I have. Missy works there."

"Yes, she does. I found out a few weeks later when I went through the drive thru. Who do I see handing me my latte? The little tart I saw making out with Erik on his porch." Stacia's expression seemed a cross between anger and satisfaction. "I said to her, 'Hey, aren't you Erik Shelton's sister-in-law?' She said she was."

"Did you confront her?"

Stacia shook her head. "What would be the point? If she's his sister-in-law, she knows who he is—*what* he is—and she's choosing it. Me going off on her only makes me look like a crazy bitch."

"So, what did you do?"

"Took my latte, smiled, and drove away without leaving a tip."

I imagined the scene, including the mild confusion it must have caused Missy. Did she start to wonder about Erik at that point? Realize being his mistress wasn't an exclusive position?

"When was that?" I asked.

"When I went through the coffee place? Two, three weeks ago."

"You're sure?"

She nodded. "Of course. It was right around the same time I made the call to his wife."

"Just so I'm clear—did you tell her about Missy?" I asked.

She cocked her head and gave me an odd look. "Of course, I did. I think that's way worse than him seeing me, don't you?"

The defeated image of Laura Shelton in the picture on my phone flashed through my mind. "I do," I agreed, letting her words sink in.

"Is that all?" Stacia asked. "Because the Zam's almost finished and I've got the second game, so..."

"No more questions," I said, and motioned for her to go. "Thank you. You've been very helpful."

36

I caught Kitty's Koffee Korner at a bit of a lull. Only a couple of customers sat in the small cafe portion, and the drive thru was empty. Missy stood behind the counter, chatting with Dania. When she saw me, a slight smile began on her lips then melted into concern.

"Is everything okay?" she asked when I reached the counter.

I glanced at Dania then motioned toward Missy. "Let's talk outside."

The two women exchanged a look, before Dania said, "Go ahead. I'll cover."

I didn't wait, but turned and walked out of the coffee shop.

Missy joined me out front, still wearing her barista apron. "What happened?" she asked.

"I should have seen it," I said. "It was right there."

"Seen what?"

"I took all the concern, and the affection, as family members bonding over grief or worry. Instead of seeing it for what it was."

233

She shook her head in confusion, though I thought I could see some worry creeping into her eyes. "You're not making sense."

"How long have you been having an affair with Erik?" I asked.

Her mouth dropped open. At the same time, her eyes flared wide. "I'm... I'm not," she stammered. "How could you say—"

"I have a witness who saw the two of you kissing on his porch."

She glanced away and back again. "We're family," she said haltingly. "I mean, of course, we hug each other and sometimes kiss. That's what families do."

"It wasn't that kind of kissing," I said. I shook my head sternly. "Missy, there's no point in lying about it."

"I'm not ly—"

"You hired me to find your sister, didn't you?"

She gave me a tentative nod. "Yes, but..."

"Do you want me to find her?"

"Of course."

"Well, you lying to me about you and Erik, or anything else, only hurts that effort." I stared at her, unrelenting. "Tell me the truth."

Missy met my gaze steadily for about three seconds. Then her lower lip trembled and she burst into tears. Her hands flew up to her face as she sobbed.

I guided her to one of the chairs at an outdoor table. She sat down but continued to sob. I settled into the chair opposite her and waited. Missy cried for several minutes before the sobs tapered off. She withdrew some napkins from her apron and wiped at her eyes and blew her nose. Then she looked over at me hesitantly.

"You must think I'm a horrible person," she said, her voice thick from tears.

"I'm not paid to make value judgments," I told her. "In this case, my goal is finding your sister. So, tell me what happened."

"What do you mean? I don't know what happened. One day, she was here. Then I found out about how she stole money from her boss. A few days later, she disappeared."

"Where did she go?"

"I told you, I don't know."

"Why did you come to Harrity's office, then?"

She glanced away from me, staring down at her hands. "I was talking with Dania, like I told you before. She said how I was Laura's only family, aside from Erik. That I needed to protect my position."

"Your position? What's that mean?" Even when I'd spoken to Dania, she couldn't really define what her biggest concern was.

Missy sighed and dabbed at her eyes again. "Honestly, I don't really know. It's something Dania said and I repeated. No one really asked me what it meant."

I peered more closely at her. "Then why did you *really* come to see Harrity?"

Missy didn't meet my gaze. She stared off into the distance, looking as if she was trying to burst into tears again.

"I didn't mean for it to start," she said, in a croaking voice. "Erik can be charming, and he made me feel special, and—"

"You know you're not the only one, right?" I said, a little surprised at how sharp my tone was.

Missy pressed her lips tight and swallowed. "I knew there were others before me. He said being with me changed all of that. He stopped seeing those other women."

"He lied," I said bluntly.

Missy took a long, wavering breath and let it out. "I sorta suspected as much. I didn't have any proof. I didn't know." A lone tear sprang from her left eye and shot down her cheek. She lifted the napkin and wiped it away. "I suppose I didn't *want* to know."

"Did Laura know about the two of you?"

Missy shook her head.

"Are you sure she didn't find out?"

Missy hesitated then shook her head again. "If she knew, she would have said something to me."

Or it could have been the last straw, I thought. The final blow convincing her to go on the run without a word.

My mind whirred with possibilities.

If she went to the cabin and Erik found her there the next day...

"I should have said something to her," sobbed Missy. More tears sprang to her eyes. "I mean, I never should have been doing that in the first place but, once I did, I should have told her. I shouldn't have kept lying to her. When I think of her not knowing and then…" She trailed off.

"Then what?" I pressed.

She didn't answer right away. First, she pressed the tissue to her eyes again and let out a long sigh. "Erik has an angry streak," she said quietly. "It's not a wide one, but it runs deep. I saw it when he found out about the money Laura stole. Sales had been slow at the dealership so—"

"Wait," I said. "Do you think Erik hurt Laura because of the money?"

Her face pinched again, another sob threatening. "I don't know," she whined. "He asked her about it and, when she said it was all gone, he didn't believe her. I asked him why she would lie and he got mad at me, too. That was when I started to worry."

"About Erik," I said, not really asking.

She nodded anyway. "He was angry all the time during those few days after everything came out. Then she disappeared. I couldn't help but worry…" She stopped short of saying it, so I finished for her.

"If he killed her," I said.

Missy swallowed hard and nodded once. "That's why I went to your boss, the lawyer. Not because of what Dania said, but because I had to know. Know for Laura's sake. If it turned out that he did, then…"

"Then you might be next."

She dipped her chin again.

"Why not go to the police?"

Her eyes widened. "I couldn't do that. What if he didn't do it?"

I stared at her in surprise. How short-sighted was this woman? "Do you see yourself with Erik at the end of all this? Is that it?"

Missy lowered her gaze to her hands once again. "No. Or maybe. I don't know anymore." She raised her eyes to mine. "It's more important to find Laura. That's what matters."

"I agree," I said quietly.

We sat in silence for a few moments. Then something Stacia mentioned struck me. "Tell me about the lake cabin," I said.

"What do you want to know? They have a cabin up at Deer Lake, that's all."

Another thought occurred to me. "Did they buy it recently?"

"You mean with the money she took?" Missy shook her head. "No, our grandparents left it to her years ago."

Of course. It couldn't be that straightforward. Nothing about this case was easy. "Could Laura be hiding there?"

Missy shook her head again. "I thought of that already. But no."

"Are you sure?"

"I went up there to check the day after she went missing. The place was locked up and quiet. She definitely wasn't there."

"If she was hiding…"

"She'd open up for me," Missy said.

"Not if she found out about you and Erik."

A sad smile lighted on her mouth. "Even more so, if that were the case." She shook her head. "No, she wasn't at the cabin."

"Did you tell the cops about the cabin?"

"Of course."

"That you'd been up there?"

"Yes."

I wondered why Detective Dow hadn't mentioned the cabin. The only reason that made sense was she'd run down the lead and found nothing. Like Missy before her, Dow didn't find Laura at the cabin.

Unless…

"Are you certain she wasn't there?" I asked.

Missy looked confused. "I already said…"

"I know what you said." I watched her carefully while she processed my implied accusation. I could envision a scenario where Missy went up to the cabin, found Laura hiding there, and warned her the police might be coming. Then Laura left before Dow arrived.

Laura seemed like a smart person. She would have to know the cabin would be one of the first places people would look, right after her own house. It didn't make sense to run straight to the second-most-likely hiding place.

"She wasn't there," Missy repeated firmly.

"I believe you."

"It doesn't sound like it."

"Is the cabin right on the lake?" I asked, ignoring her comment.

"No. It's a few minutes' walk away from the water. Why?"

"How big is the property?"

"Just a single lot," Missy said.

"Like a residential neighborhood, or...?"

She shook her head. "There's some BLM land behind the secondary lots that don't sit on the lake itself. People like to hike or ride horses back there. Why?"

I didn't answer. Instead, I asked, "Where's Erik right now?"

"Still at the hospital," said Missy. "They're supposed to call me later today when he's released."

"Don't pick him up," I told her.

"Why?"

I gave her a pointed look. "You went to see Harrity because you were worried he might have been capable of killing your sister, or you. Do I have to spell out the rest for you?"

Turns out, I didn't.

37

I got the address for the lake cabin from Missy and headed home. I needed to think these revelations over for a bit. In my past, I've frequently gone crashing forward at the first hint of a possible solution to a case or situation. That approach has resulted in plenty of trouble for me. Even when it hadn't, when I look back, I saw that, in most of those instances, I could have waited and considered first and not lost momentum.

At home, I made a sandwich and ate it slowly, thinking about everything I'd learned. My suspicions about Erik had grown, but was he capable of murder? It was difficult to say. Missy clearly thought so. Of course, if she truly believed it, wouldn't she have gone to the police?

I realized the answer was no. She *did* believe him capable of murder; otherwise, she'd never have come to Harrity's office. She just didn't *want* to believe it. That's what kept her from reporting her concerns to Dow.

My thought process strung together several tenuous *ifs*. *If* Laura was murdered and wasn't simply on the run, and *if* Erik was the murderer, wouldn't the forested area behind the lake cabin make for a convenient place to hide the body?

If, if, if.

I couldn't make an accusation on this many inconclusive facts.

I stood and paced through the house. My next move had to be going up to the lake cabin, didn't it? I wondered if there was anything else I should do first. My clearest options were to consult with Harrity, or report what I had to Detective Dow. Somehow, neither seemed like it would result in anything worthwhile. If I went that route, *maybe* Dow would be the one to go up to the cabin instead of me if she chose to follow up at all. More likely, it was a lead she'd probably already checked on.

She must have, I decided. Anything less would be negligent. That meant there'd definitely been no Laura at the cabin.

But it didn't mean Laura's body…

You, of all people, should know stories like hers don't have a happy ending.

I shook my head at the thought. I didn't want to find Laura's shallow grave in the woods. Let someone else do that.

Doubt crept in as I paced. The cabin was probably just another dead end. Something Dow already checked. Then again, Missy had lied once…

I paused at the front window. Across the street, in the park, I spotted Mick Darabont, reading a book and waiting for a checkers opponent. That seemed like a pleasant diversion, so I exited the house and trudged across the street. When I drew near to him, Mick lowered his paperback and looked up at me.

"Back for another round?" he asked.

"Thought I might give it a try."

I settled into the bench. Mick turned the board around so the black pieces were on my side this time. I glanced up at him.

The old man just stared back at me. "Fair is fair," he grunted. "I went first last time."

I reached out and moved the first checker, and we played.

The game moved quickly at first, then slowed down. There were only a few possible moves available each turn, so I took the time to examine each before committing. Even so, he soon had me hemmed in and playing a defensive game. After ten minutes or so, my pieces were depleted and I was buried deep onto my side of the board.

I sat back and rubbed my eyes. "You're kicking my ass," I lamented.

"You're holding up better than last time."

"That's because you gave me black."

He shrugged. "Seemed like the only fair choice."

"Owed me after last time, huh?" I joked.

Mick shook his head. "Nobody owes anybody anything but the truth." He slid a checker forward, boxing in one of mine so no matter which way I moved, he'd jump it. Then he looked up at me. "Sometimes not even that."

It took less than five more minutes for him to

jump my last checker, but his words haunted me
long after that.

38

After my ignominious defeat at Mick's hands, I walked back across the street to my house. The more I thought about the situation, the clearer my next move became.

I had to go to the cabin.

Maybe Missy told the truth about Laura not being there but, if Erik was the killer, the nearby woods provided his best place to hide the body. He had easy access. No one would be suspicious of his presence. It was remote enough the body may not be found for decades, or ever.

Before I could change my mind, I got into the car and started north. Deer Lake was about ten minutes north of Deer Park, where I grew up. Deer Park was about twenty minutes north of River City, up Highway 395. Once I got past the north end of the city, houses became sparse and the highway opened up. I was halfway to Deer Park before another thought occurred to me.

I fished my phone out of my pocket and dialed. After six rings, Erik answered.

"Hello?" he said, his voice slightly groggy.

"It's Stefan Kopriva."

"So?"

"Can you drive?" I asked.

"What the hell?"

"Can you drive?" I repeated, more forcefully. "Or are you on meds?"

"I can drive," he grunted. "What do you care?"

"I'm headed up to your cabin at Deer Lake," I told him.

"You're *what?*"

"Meet me there and let's end this."

"You son of a—"

I hung up.

For the rest of the drive, I thought over my decision. If Erik wasn't the killer, it would be good to have him there. He could open up the cabin and tell me if anything was amiss. If he *was* the killer? Given that he'd just left the hospital after the beating he took from Tyler, I felt confident I could handle him physically.

Out of caution, I popped open the glove box. Inside, the stainless steel of my Kahr forty-caliber reflected in the sunlight that came through the car window. I reached in, grabbed it, and tucked it into the small of my back again.

Just in case.

39

The Shelton cabin wasn't too hard to find. The main road near the lake was paved. Fruit Tree Lane, where the cabin was located, was an offshoot of the main road. The first quarter mile was gravel then it turned to dirt. Fruit Tree Lane seemed to run somewhat parallel to the main road, so the distance to the lake remained roughly the same.

A simple wooden sign with white stenciled letters announced the address for the cabin. I slowed for the sharp turn into the driveway. The cabin was another thirty yards up a slight incline.

There were no other cars in view. The cabin was painted a rusty red. Actually, calling it a cabin was a misnomer. In appearance, it was more of a bungalow, a smaller version of any house you might see in a middle-class neighborhood in River City. Closer up, the red paint was peeling slightly and dull white paint adorned the trim. A raised porch ran along the entire front of the cabin, complete with a hammock at one end and a pair of Adirondack chairs at the other. A tiny, free-standing garage stood nearby.

I stopped directly in front of the cabin and shut off my car.

I sat for a moment, listening. All I could hear was the slow ticking as my engine cooled, the slight rustle of wind through the nearby pines, and a few stray bird calls.

When I got out of the car, the thudding sound of my car door slamming shut seemed to echo throughout the property. I waited a moment to see if it would provoke a reaction from anyone.

Nothing.

I shuffled to the garage first. A metal latch with a keyed handle adorned the roll-up door. I tried it but it was locked. Through a small window on the side, I could see the outline of a battered old Jeep inside.

I made my way to the front door. The top half of the door was essentially a window. I peered through the glass. The sheer white curtains on the inside warped my view of the interior but I could see well enough to know there was no one in the room. The cabin seemed still.

I tried the door, but it was locked. In some circumstances, I might be tempted to force it, but Erik was on his way, so I didn't. Instead, I wandered around the outside of the building. The curtains were drawn on some of the windows but I was able to look through a couple. I saw no sign of anyone.

Around the back, I found a woodcutting station under a lean-to. A stack of split wood sat against the wall. An axe was stuck into the over-sized stump used as a cutting block. There was some debris near the stump that clearly wasn't fresh, but I couldn't tell if it was days or even months old. The downside to being a city kid, apparently.

The rear windows were mostly shrouded by curtains. Up higher than the rest, a smaller rectangular window was cracked open an inch. I might have found that interesting if not for the fact that, even if I could get up to the window, I'd barely be able to fit an arm through it, much less squeeze inside.

By the time I emerged at the front of the cabin, I didn't know anything more than when I arrived. I thought about taking a walk around the wooded area behind the cabin, and decided against it. Would I even recognize a burial site if I stumbled across it? Unless the earth was freshly turned, I doubted it.

No, if Erik was the killer, my better course of action was to get him to admit it. He could lead the police to where he buried his wife.

I walked onto the porch and took a seat in one of the large chairs next to a large potted plant littered with crushed cigarette butts, and waited.

Erik arrived about twenty minutes later. He roared up the driveway in his Mustang, sliding to a stop less than a foot away from my old Celica. The door to his car flung open and hung there a moment before he climbed out gingerly. His face was still battered and bruised, but I could see the snarl of his expression.

He walked slowly but purposefully toward me.

"What the fuck are you doing here?" he growled.

His hands were empty, I noticed, except for his keys. His right arm was still splinted and cradled in a sling. All the same, I leaned forward slightly to provide quick access to the small of my back in case I needed my gun.

"This seemed like the most appropriate place to put an end to the mystery," I said.

He neared the porch steps. "The hell?"

"Come on, Erik," I said, waving my hand at the surrounding trees. "This is the perfect place to hide a body, isn't it?"

He stopped suddenly, one foot on the first step to the porch, his gaze fixed on me. The one eye that had been swollen shut yesterday was open to a slit today, so this time both of his eyes burned at me.

"Are you *kidding* me?" he asked. "You think I killed my wife?"

"You didn't?"

"No!" He shook his head, dumbfounded. "Why would I?"

"I'd like to know the answer to that," I said. "If you're asking for my operating theory, there are several possibilities."

"You're crazy," he said.

I ignored and pressed on. "Could be, when you found out about the money she'd stolen, you wanted it. Or maybe you needed it. Missy said work wasn't going so great. Either way, Laura wouldn't—

or couldn't—give it to you, so you killed her."

"Get real, dude."

"Or she found out about your affair with Stacia and was going to leave, along with the money. So, you killed her."

"This is ridiculous. I told you, we had an under—"

"Or," I said, interrupting him, "she found out you've been banging her sister, threatened to leave you and take her money with her, so you killed her."

Erik's eyes flared open in surprise.

"Missy told me everything," I said. "At least, everything she knew."

"She's lying," Erik whispered, but there was no conviction in his voice.

"She told me what she suspected, too," I said. "About you. Which is why we're here now."

Erik shook his head, anger and disbelief etched on his face.

"Tell me the truth, Erik," I said. "Let's end this."

"*I didn't kill her*," Erik said, his jaw clenched so tightly his lips barely moved.

"Then where is she?"

"I don't know."

"Why did the two of you fight that last night you saw her?"

I could hear Erik's breath from where I sat as he drew it in through his mouth. He stared at me with some surprise but also with what looked like naked hatred. "You piece of shit," he muttered. "You can't just *accuse* someone like that. It's not right."

"What was the fight about?" I repeated.

He stared hard at me. "What do you think? The money and Missy."

"Let's start with the money. What was that argument about?"

"That she took it," Erik said. "That she didn't tell me. How we were going to get sued and lose everything."

"What else?"

"That's it."

"Come on, Erik. Story time is over. You argued about where the money was, didn't you?"

He hesitated.

"Tell me," I urged.

"We talked about that," he admitted.

"Did she tell you where the money was?"

"She said it was gone. That she spent it."

"*All* of it?"

He nodded slowly.

"You didn't believe her, did you?"

He stared at me for a few seconds then shrugged. "I don't know if it was that I didn't believe her, or just didn't want to believe she was going to go to prison for stealing money that was now all gone."

"You know you wouldn't get to keep the money anyway, right?"

He gave me a confused look. "They couldn't just take it. I mean, they'd have to prove it was the money she took, wouldn't they?"

"It's the other way around," I said. "If they could find anything that even resembled the stolen funds, they'd freeze the account. You'd be more likely to lose some of your legitimate money than to get your hands on what she embezzled."

His eyes narrowed. "Are you sure? That sounds like a violation of my rights."

"Which rights are those?"

"I don't know," he mumbled, glancing away. "Privacy or something?"

"Is that what happened?" I asked him. "You got angry after you found out the money was gone? Or because you thought she was lying about that?"

"Of course, I got mad," Erik snapped. "We got into it. Then she brought up Missy."

"Not the old news, like you told me."

Erik shrugged. "You didn't need to know my business."

"Tell me about the Missy part," I said.

"There's nothing much to tell. She accused me. I denied, told her she had no proof other than some crazy rumor. Then she left."

"Did she come back later that night?"

"No."

"When did you see her again?"

"I haven't seen her since that night," Erik said, emphasizing each word. "She disappeared."

"What did she take with her when she left the house?"

"Nothing."

"Not one single thing?"

"Well, her purse, I think." He thought about it for a second then said, "Yeah, I remember because she went into the bedroom to get it. She was in there for a little while and I thought maybe she was going to hole up in there, but she came out, grabbed her keys, and left."

"When we first spoke, you told me you cut the argument short to go play hockey. Now, you're saying she left first. Which is it?"

"She left," Erik insisted. "Then I went to my game."

"Why lie to me about it?"

He shrugged. "I guess I remembered it differently before, that's all."

"That's called lying," I said. "It's at least the second lie you told me that day."

"Go to hell," Erik snapped, pointing a finger at me. "I didn't hurt her!"

"Then where is she?"

"I don't know! I didn't do anything to her."

I stared at him, trying to gauge the sincerity of his outrage. He was very convincing, but I reminded myself he was a used car salesman.

"Do you really think she's…?" Erik trailed off, seemingly unwilling to finish the thought.

"Dead?" I said, watching for his reaction.

Pain flashed in his eyes. He nodded dumbly.

"The detective assigned to the case thinks so," I said.

"But… who would…?"

"You tell me."

Erik turned to stare out at the nearby trees, seeming to give the question due consideration.

Finally, he turned back to me.

"It was the old man's daughter," he said, his tone convinced. "That's why she sent her bruiser of a boyfriend after me."

"What did he say to you when he…?"

"When he beat the shit out of me?" Erik asked, resentment dripping from every word.

This time, it was me who nodded without a word.

"He kept going between threatening to sue and asking where the money was," Erik said.

"Did you tell him?"

"How could I? I don't know where Laura hid it." Erik shrugged. "Or maybe she really did spend it all."

"Did you tell him that?"

"Of course."

"He didn't take your word for it, did he?"

Erik lifted his splinted arm slightly, flicking his fingers toward his bruised face, and let it drop. "What do you think?"

I sat quietly for a few seconds, thinking. In the distance, I could hear tires crunching gravel then falling almost silent as the road turned to dirt. I kept my eyes fixed on Erik's expression looking for a crack in his facade, but none came.

He was telling the truth.

"Why would Rena or Tyler kill Laura?"

"They must have wanted the money," Erik said.

I thought about my earlier accusation and how Rena reacted. It'd been a stab in the dark to accuse her and resulted in much the same outcome as my accusation of Erik. But my reasoning for why Rena might have done it remained sound. She could have been angry about Laura's actions, whether because it delayed her father's retirement or impacted her own position. It could have simply been out of jealousy, feeling threatened by Laura usurping her role as a daughter.

Her response to me rang in my ears.

Oh, yes, I killed Laura and buried her in the woods.

That admission had been heavily laden with sarcasm. Did she use that to veil the truth?

"Tyler," I muttered, another thought occurring to me. "Is it possible, this whole time, she's been afraid of him?"

"What?" Erik asked. He stepped up onto the porch, coming closer to me.

I glanced at him. "If Rena did something to Laura and Tyler knew about it, he'd have leverage over her. Plus, he's already proven he's a violent person. Maybe she's the one under duress of some kind."

"Duress?" Erik shook his head. "She doesn't seem like the kind of person anyone could intimidate. She's more the type who does the intimidating."

"Maybe," I admitted. "If she's being blackmailed…"

"Is this what you do?" Erik asked, waving his free hand in my direction. "Sit around and speculate like some kind of crazy conspiracy theorist?"

"No. Usually, I have more evidence to go on."

"So, you just accuse people instead?"

I met his gaze. "Put yourself in my shoes, Erik. Watch a few episodes of any true crime reality show. You can't see how you're a prime suspect?"

He wanted to say no, I could tell but, after a few moments, he sighed. "That's some *bull*shit," he muttered.

I opened my mouth to reply when the nose of a Dodge Charger appeared in the driveway.

"Damn," I breathed, recognizing it almost immediately.

"What?" Erik turned to follow my gaze. "Who's that?"

"Tyler Driggs," I told him and pushed myself to my feet.

40

We both watched Tyler stop his car near the end of the driveway and get out.

"How'd he…?" Erik said, his voice confused.

"He must have followed you," I said.

Erik glanced at me, his eyes narrowing. "Maybe he followed *you.*"

"Maybe," I shrugged, "but he showed up after you got here."

Erik opened his mouth to argue and stopped. Then he muttered a curse. As we watched Tyler stride confidently toward us, Erik held up his keys suddenly. "Wait. There's a shotgun inside, in the bedroom closet."

"No time," I said. "Besides…" I motioned toward his splinted arm.

Erik glanced down. When he looked up, he was frowning. He slipped the keys into his front pocket and pulled his phone from his back one. For most of my life, that was where men carried their wallets but, more and more, it was for phones.

"Shit, no signal," Erik said. "As usual."

I didn't answer him. Tyler Driggs was nearly to the rear of Erik's Mustang now. I angled my body slightly, and waited.

Tyler stopped once he got clear of the vehicles. He ignored me and stared at Erik. "We want our fucking money back," he said, matter-of-factly. "Or more of what you got is on the way."

Before Erik could answer, I said, "Not scratching cars or leaving notes today, Tyler?"

Tyler's face hardened but a smirk played underneath. "I don't know what you mean."

"You should leave. There's a felony warrant out for you."

"So?" Tyler scoffed. He pointed at Erik. "That won't stop me from getting our money."

"The cops will find you eventually," I told him.

"The cops couldn't find pussy at a whorehouse," Tyler jeered. He pointed at me. "You need to mind your own fucking business."

"You should leave while you can," I said.

Tyler ignored me and looked around at the cabin and its surroundings. "This is nice," he said. "Did you two buy this with all the money that bitch stole?"

"Don't talk about her like that," Erik said.

Tyler smirked. "What are you going to do? Huh? Nothing, that's what." He looked some more, admiring the setting. Then his gaze hardened and fell on Erik again. "You hid the money here, didn't you?"

"I don't know what she did with the money," Erik told him.

"Sure, you do," Tyler said easily. He pointed

toward the cabin door. "Let's go inside and you can show me."

"I don't have your money," Erik insisted.

"We'll go inside," Tyler continued, ignoring his denial. "You'll give me the money and, if enough of it is still left, I won't kick your ass again."

"There's no money."

"Sure there is." Tyler took a step forward.

"You're not going inside," said Erik.

Tyler paused. A smug, dangerous smile spread across his mouth. "Oh, I am going inside. There's no doubt of that. The only question is if you want to show me around or wait out here on the porch, bleeding."

"You're not going—" Erik started to say again, but Tyler ignored him and stepped forward.

I drew my pistol and leveled it at him.

"Stop right there!" I barked, summoning up the commanding tone I'd used all those years ago on the job.

Surprise briefly lighted on Tyler's face. Then his smug confidence returned. "Put that away," he said. "You're not going to shoot me."

"Try me," I said firmly.

Tyler crossed his arms and stared at me. "You do and you'll go to prison for the rest of your life."

"Do you know where you are?" I asked him.

He glanced around. "At a fucking lake cabin. What's your point?"

"You're in Stevens County," I said.

"So?"

"So, this isn't River City. There is no police department. Up here, it's the Sheriff's Office."

Tyler uncrossed his arms and turned over his hands. "So?" he repeated, his tone exasperated.

"So, they see different kinds of cases up here. They look at situations differently than in the city. Up here," I waved at our surroundings with my left hand and returned it to support my gun hand, "what the deputy who responds will see is a dead man on someone else's property. A dead man with a felony warrant, who attacked the homeowner. Someone he'd previously assaulted only a couple of days prior. He'll see a dead man shot with a legally owned firearm by someone who was reasonably in fear for his own safety and that of the homeowner."

Tyler smirked at me. "I'm unarmed."

I shrugged. "Based on your violence against Erik and my knowledge that you're a trained fighter, there's more than enough justification."

"You're willing to bet your freedom on being right about that?" Tyler asked.

"That's not the question," I said, keeping my gun aimed at his chest. "The question is, are you willing to bet your life on whether I believe it?"

He glared at me. "It's prison, motherfucker. For the rest of your life."

"Or not," I said, motioning toward Erik with my head. "We're on his property, remember?"

"It doesn't work that way, asshole."

I shrugged. "Even if I'm wrong, it won't matter to you if you're dead."

Tyler's hot, appraising stare burned into me. I could tell he wanted to test my resolve. He wanted to believe I was bluffing, to tear into the both of us, and then tear apart the cabin to find the money he surely thought was inside.

I kept my finger indexed along the side of the pistol, waiting. If he came toward us, I'd put my finger on the trigger. If he reached the porch steps, I'd shoot.

I wasn't bluffing.

It was up to Tyler to find out.

We stood in silence, all three of us. Only the whisper of the wind and the soft call of birds surrounded us, coupled with that same eerie quiet I'd noticed upon my arrival. Tyler stared at me, bristling with fury. I returned his gaze, at peace with my decision. He might be right about how this would turn out in a court of law, but I was willing to take my chances.

It took nearly a minute before Tyler broke first. He didn't move, but he recrossed his arms and leaned back slightly. That alone told me I'd won the standoff. Then, he said, "Fine but you know I'll be back." He jabbed a finger at Erik. "You're going to give us back our money, asshole."

"I don't have it," Erik said softly.

"Hell you don't," said Tyler. "I'll come back another day and —"

"You're not going anywhere," I said, my gun still leveled at Tyler's chest.

Tyler's eyes cut to mine. "The fuck are you

talking about?"

I motioned toward Erik. "He's going to call the cops. You're staying right here with us until they get here. Then they're going to take you in on your warrant."

Tyler followed my gesture then returned his gaze to me.

"What if I turn and walk back to my car instead?" he challenged. "What are you gonna do? Shoot me?"

"Yes, I'll shoot you," I agreed.

Tyler gave me the same appraising look as before, except it was cooler this time. After a few seconds, he shook his head. "No," he said. "You just blew past your exit, hotshot."

I didn't answer, just kept my gun pointed toward him.

"You might be able to sell that other load of crap you were saying before to the hick cops up here," Tyler said. "Shooting me in the back as I walk away ain't gonna fly with anyone."

"You're a dangerous felon," I reminded him.

"You ain't a cop," he said.

"That doesn't matter," I lied.

"It's all that matters," Tyler said.

"Maybe I'll just shoot you where you stand, then."

Tyler spread his arms. "Then do it, motherfucker."

I stood for a moment then lowered the pistol. "You better get going," I suggested. "The cops will be here in a few minutes."

His smug expression returned. "Good luck calling them," he said. "There's no way you get reception up here."

I thought he might take a step forward to test me again. His hard eyes threatened such an action. Instead he turned on his heels and walked straight back toward his Charger without a backward glance.

"Holy shit," Erik breathed, keeping his voice low. "Would you really have shot him?"

"Yes," I said.

Erik cast a look down the driveway before answering. "Good," he whispered, almost to himself.

We watched Tyler as he reached his car. He fired a middle finger at both of us before he got inside. The engine rumbled to life and he revved it loudly. Then he spun the tires as he backed out of the driveway and accelerated up the road. Only then did I return my gun to the small of my back.

"Holy shit," Erik repeated. "He's crazy." He glanced over at me. "Wait. You don't really think he could have… that him and his girlfriend…?"

I shrugged. "Maybe. I don't know."

Erik shook his head in amazement. "I should have known. After the way he jumped me…"

"We need to call the cops," I said. "He might come back. Who knows, maybe they can nab him in Deer Park or on 395."

"Right," Erik said. He lifted his phone and shook

his head. "Still no service."

"Is there a landline in the cabin?"

"No." He swallowed, his tone hesitant. "I could go down to the store. There's a cafe attached and they've got good cell coverage there."

"You don't sound like you want to do that."

"I don't want to meet that crazy bastard again."

"I wouldn't worry about that. If he was going to push things, he'd have done it here. At this point, I suspect he's headed toward the highway."

"You sure?"

"No. But what else are we going to do? Stand here all day?"

Erik frowned. "Yeah, I guess you're right." He took a deep breath and steeled himself. "All right, I'll go."

"Okay." I motioned toward the door to the cabin. "You think I could get some water while I wait?"

"Sure," Erik said. He pulled out his keys and unlocked the door. "I'll be back in ten minutes or so."

"All right. You mind if I look around a little?"

Erik shrugged. "Knock yourself out. I've got nothing to hide. No one's been up here in months." He walked toward his car, got in, and jockeyed back and forth a couple of times so he could head down the driveway.

I watched his car until he made the left turn and disappeared. Then I pushed open the cabin door and stepped inside.

41

The inside of the cabin didn't smell as musty as I expected. The scent of split firewood hung heavily in the air, riding underneath the distinct odor of woodsmoke. A third smell teased my nostrils, making me think immediately of my mother. A moment later, I recognized it—the stale hint of cigarette smoke.

Glancing around, I noticed several chunks of firewood stacked in an iron rack near a wood stove. I held my hand above the black metal and felt no heat. I slowly lowered my fingers to touch the stove. The metal frame was cool.

I wandered toward the small kitchen. There were no dishes in the twin sinks, though a few sat on the plastic drying rack next to them. I glanced closer at them but saw no water. No dust, either.

I found the glasses in the second cupboard I opened. The kitchen faucet kicked on without any hiccups from air in the lines. I filled the glass and drank it down. The water was cold and tasted good, making me realize the place was probably on a well system.

For a while, I stood in the kitchen, holding the empty glass and listening to the various small noises the cabin made. Nothing sounded out of the ordinary. My mind drifted back to the confrontation with Tyler and I wondered whether he'd be dumb enough to get back on Highway 395 and head to Spokane. In that Dodge Charger, a state trooper ought to be able to lay in wait, spotting him easily enough.

Then what?

I turned on the faucet and filled the glass halfway, sipping this time. If Detective Dow got a shot at interviewing Tyler, would he break?

Thinking about his cold, hard eyes, I doubted it. Not if he'd killed Laura on Rena's behalf. He'd take his chances with a trial before he'd confess.

What if Rena did the deed, and Tyler only knew about it? That changed the dynamics considerably. Now, he was in a position of greater strength. He had some leverage. Dow could get the prosecutor to agree to a lighter sentence on the assault charge in exchange for information and his testimony in the murder case. Hell, Erik himself might force the issue if he found out, by simply refusing to press charges in the assault if Tyler would give up Rena.

I took another sip of the water, then dumped out the rest.

It was a whole lot of ifs, which had been the story of this case since the beginning.

If they caught Tyler.

If Rena was the killer.

If Tyler would turn on his girlfriend.

Hell, *if* she was even dead, and not already in Mexico, like Rena suggested.

I put the glass in the sink and decided to check out the remainder of the small cabin. There was a bedroom off the kitchen. The single queen bed was made. I didn't bother with the closet or the single chest of drawers. Instead, I pushed open the connecting bathroom door. The small window I'd seen from the outside was open a crack.

When I stepped inside, I noticed a shift in humidity. A small zing shot up my spine. Cautiously, I reached out toward the shower curtain and nudged it aside.

Nothing.

Except…

I leaned closer to look and touched the bottom of the curtain to be sure.

It was damp.

Someone had used the shower within the last few hours.

I stood upright, glancing around for hiding places. The only possibility in the bathroom was a large cupboard. I popped it open and looked inside. Folded towels filled the space. I closed the cupboard and moved to the bedroom. Carefully lowering myself to my knees, I dropped onto my stomach and looked under the bed.

No one.

I pushed myself up to my knees and stood again. The nearby closet door seemed like the next best location to try, so I walked toward it and tugged on the knob. There was some resistance, but it felt odd, not like the usual rattle of a locked door. Instead, it seemed somehow more elastic, with more initial give before it settled back into the latch.

Like someone was holding the knob.

I took a deep breath and gave it another forceful pull. This time it flew open without resistance. My own force caused me to stagger backward half a step, windmilling slightly with my free hand to retain my balance.

In that moment, my eyes met those of a dark-haired woman standing inside the closet.

Laura Shelton.

42

Before I could utter a word, Laura snapped up a shotgun, pointing it directly at my chest.

"Who the hell are you?" she demanded.

I raised my hands reflexively. "Easy. I'm Stefan Kopriva."

"I don't know you. What are you doing in my house?"

"Your sister hired me."

Confusion seeped into her expression. "Missy?"

I nodded. "She hired me to find you."

"She…" Laura shook her head, as if to clear it. "It doesn't matter. Back away."

I walked backward several steps. Laura advanced toward me, still pointing the shotgun at me.

"Out there," she said, motioning toward the bedroom door.

We marched methodically out of the bedroom and into the larger kitchen and living room area, me shuffling backward with my hands raised, and her creeping forward with the shotgun barrel never wavering from my midsection.

"Stop," she ordered.

I did as she said.

Laura eyed me for several long seconds, obviously processing what I'd told her. I waited, taking in her appearance. She looked harried and tired. Her expression had a frantic edge to it, which made perfect sense to me for someone on the run. In that moment, she looked much closer to that photo on my phone than the one I'd taken from the wall. There was no light in her eyes, only haggard suspicion and deep desperation. There was no bloom, as Clell had described her inner beauty.

"How'd you find me?"

"Missy told me about the cabin. I came to check it out."

She stared at me, as if parsing my words for the truth. Then she said, "Do you have a phone?"

I nodded.

"Take it out," she ordered.

Slowly, I reached into my pocket and removed my cell phone. The weight of my Kahr forty-caliber shifted with my movement, but I never considered trying to draw it out. Instead, I held up the phone for her to see.

"Put it there." She dipped toward the kitchen table with the shotgun's barrel.

I set the phone on the table.

"Now back away," she said. "All the way into the living room."

I stepped slowly backwards. "Laura…"

"Shut up," she snapped. She reached out with

one hand and picked up my phone. The shotgun barrel fell downward as she hurriedly slid the phone into her pocket. She quickly returned her hand to the fore-stock, lifting the barrel again. Then she shuffled forward a few feet and jabbed toward one of the chairs opposite the wood stove. "Sit down."

I did as she said, lowering myself into the chair. I was careful to keep my hands on the chair arms. "Laura, it's over," I said, keeping my voice as calm as I could.

"Don't talk to me like you know me," she said.

"I feel like I do, a little."

"Well, you don't." She began circling toward the front door. When she drew close, she cast a hurried glance out the window before snapping her gaze back to me. "Where's Erik? I heard his voice before."

"He went to call the cops."

"He *what?*"

"He went to the store so he could get cell service. He's calling the cops. They'll be here any minute now."

"You're lying."

I lifted my hands slightly, turning them over. "You don't have to believe me. But they'll be here soon."

Her gaze drilled into me. "Why? Why are they coming here?"

"Rena's boyfriend was here, making threats."

"Tyler?"

"He beat up Erik a couple of days ago and was

eager to go another round."

"Why?"

"He wants the money back. He and Rena are convinced Erik was in on it with you, or at least that he found out about it before you disappeared."

Laura shook her head slowly. "Erik didn't know anything until I told him."

"I figured that."

She glanced at the window in the door again, then back at me. "You stay in that chair," she warned. "I'm leaving."

"In what? That old Jeep in the garage?"

Her expression tightened. "It runs. I started it when I first got here."

"You'll be lucky to get a mile before a deputy stops you."

"Shut up." Her hand pulled away from the forestock and reached toward the knob. The gun barrel dipped again, going nearly vertical.

"Even if you get away from the lake, where are you going to go, Laura?" I projected as much sympathy into my tone as I could muster. It wasn't difficult. "How will you survive? The money's gone, isn't it?"

She gave me a sharp look.

"It is," I said. "Otherwise, you'd already be on a beach somewhere."

Laura twisted the knob. "You're just trying to stall, keep me here until the police arrive."

"I'm not trying to hide that fact," I said. "The police are your best option right now. Better than a life on the run."

Laura pulled open the door. "I'm not going to prison for that bitch," she said.

My brow wrinkled. "Who, Rena?"

She swung the door wide and brought her hand back to support the fore-stock of the shotgun. "Don't act like you care. No one cares."

I turned over my hands again. "I actually do," I said. "So does your sister."

I watched her reaction, expecting to see venom or fury. There was only hurt and betrayal. As she returned my gaze, she wavered. That told me something; she loved her sister, despite knowing about her and Erik.

"If there's more to this story than just you stealing all that money from Lawrence, you need to tell me."

"It doesn't matter." Laura backed toward the open doorway. "Stay in the chair until I leave."

"I can help you," I said. "Missy went to a criminal defense attorney I work for. He's the best in the city, and it isn't even close. Tell your story, Laura. He can help you."

"He can keep me from going to jail?" she asked.

"No," I admitted. "Probably not. He might be able to keep you out of prison, though. One of his arguments will be you turned yourself in. It looks worse if the cops have to chase you down — and they will, Laura. You're no criminal and everyone screws up eventually."

She hesitated, watching me. The gun barrel

wavered, but didn't fall. I could see resolve returning to her eyes.

"It's already too late," I said. "They'll be here any minute. Do you really want to be holding me hostage with a shotgun when they do?"

The gun barrel wavered some more, then she let it drop toward the ground. She closed the door and walked to the chair opposite the one where I sat. As she lowered herself into it, she put the shotgun across her knees.

"I'm not going to prison for her," Laura repeated.

"Then tell me what happened."

She didn't speak for at least a minute. Even though her eyes were on me, there was a slight glaze to them, as if she were deep in thought. Finally, she said, "What do you want to know?"

"All of it," I said.

43

Laura spoke slowly at first, probing me to see how much I already knew. When my foundation of understanding became apparent, she dove in to the missing parts of the story.

"I didn't start taking money from them until Lawrence said no to my partnership request for the final time," she said. "Two years ago. Before that, it never even occurred to me."

"What changed?" I asked. "I mean, besides the refusal?"

Laura let out a long breath. "I had several reasons. For one, I was in my forties, stuck in a job with a boss that didn't appreciate me."

"He told me he thought of you as another daughter."

"He said the same to me," Laura said, "but, when push came to shove, it was clear that was just lip service. Another illusion of something good in my life that actually wasn't good. In addition to the dead-end job, I was married to a cheater. It was bad enough I knew he was messing around, but the way he lied about it and tried to make me feel like I was the crazy one? It was too much. It was too late to start over. I was locked in by my own choices."

"It's never too late," I offered.

"Really?" she scoffed. She looked at me appraisingly. "You look almost my age. Are you telling me you could just up and start over? That your past and the decisions you've made would have no impact?"

I thought of the tiny grave up at Forest Lawn cemetery, a forever testament to the worst mistake of my life. Other graves and other mistakes followed that scene, a cavalcade of images, all in support of Laura's assertion.

"You don't have to answer," Laura said. "I can see it in your face." She took another deep breath and let it out. "Anyway, it seemed like I'd spent most of my life doing for others. Giving to my marriage and to Fresh Pines. Look how that turned out. I decided it was time to take a little for myself." She met my gaze. "That's when I started stealing money."

"Is that when you started with Ted?"

She tilted her head in surprise. "You found out about that?"

I nodded. "Ted finally told me. He didn't want to, but I guilted him into it."

"How?"

"I told him it might be how we find you. Or your body."

She winced slightly at the last sentence. Then she said, "That was harsh to say to him. Ted has a kind soul."

"I weighed out his hurt feelings versus finding you," I said. "You won out."

She gave me a strange look then shrugged. "Anyway, yes. That was when I started with Ted. I kept it going with him and continued taking the money for a while. The whole time, I expected to be caught at any moment. But no one figured out what Ted and I were doing or no one cared, anyway."

"The money?"

"That's the funny part of all of this," Laura said. "The only reason I got caught was because Rena was stealing money herself. She figured out what I was doing because *she* was doing it."

"Rena was embezzling, too?"

"Oh, yeah. I'd started to notice some things that weren't quite right but I was hesitant to say anything. I mean, I was stealing money myself, right? So, I asked her a couple of cautious questions. Her reaction told me I was correct about my suspicions. She must have figured out I knew, because it broke pretty quickly after that."

"You two had a confrontation?"

"She came to the office one night when I was working late. Just her. We had it out. All cards on the table. She accused me and I accused her back. We both realized we were both right. Then she made herself very clear. She was going to blame me for all the money I took *and* all the money she took."

"How long had she been stealing?"

"Way longer than me. Up to ten years or more,

as best as I could figure." She shook her head emphatically. "I might have been willing to answer for my own actions, but I was not taking responsibility for what she did."

"And Tyler...?"

"Tyler's an idiot. If I had to guess, she probably has him believing the same story as everyone else. That I took all the money and still have it."

I didn't say so, but that sounded about right to me. "Could she have gotten away with it?" I asked. "Making all the embezzlement look like it was you?"

Laura nodded mournfully. "I'm the bookkeeper. All she has to do is say I was the one who changed the paperwork. Since there are other instances where I did exactly that, what is there to differentiate between the two?"

"I don't know enough about accounting to answer that."

"You don't have to. She's the daughter, set to inherit the business. Why would she steal? I'm the accountant, the woman scorned. There are examples of embezzlement I absolutely *did* do. So, how hard is it to believe I did all of it?" She stared off into space, her fingers twitching where she still held the shotgun. "Shit. I shouldn't have listened to you. I should have gotten into the Jeep and left."

"You made the right choice," I assured her.

"Right or wrong," she said with a sigh. "I've made it."

I steered her back to her story. "What happened

next?"

Laura frowned. "It was a shit couple of days. Rena told Lawrence about the money and he called the police. He didn't even ask me if it was true. The detective called me, and I was trying to decide whether to call her back. Then I got another voice message from some woman claiming to be another one in Erik's list of infidelities. Only, she told me..."

Her voice broke.

"About Missy," I finished.

Laura swallowed. "Yes. About the two of them. I needed time to think, so I took a long walk. When I got back, Erik came at me about the money. Apparently, Lawrence called the house while I was out and told him everything. So we fought about all of it."

"You decided to leave?"

She lifted her hands and dropped them. "What was the point in staying?"

"Where'd you go?" I asked. "After the fight with Erik?"

"I went to Coeur d'Alene," she said. "I stayed at a cheap motel and tried to figure out what to do. After a week, my cash started to run out, so I decided to hide up here until I came up with a better plan."

"They found your car at Northtown Mall," I said.

"I left it there. I took the bus up to Deer Park and got a taxi up to the lake."

"Why here? You had to think people would

check this place."

"I hoped they'd already come and gone," she said. "I knew the store would give me a line of credit if I needed it. Poppa's Jeep was in the garage if I decided to run for good." She bit her lip. "Not a great plan, I know. It wasn't like I had a lot of experience hiding out from the cops."

She was right, on both counts. It wasn't a masterful strategy. But I didn't know how much better most people with her civilian background would do when faced with a similar circumstance.

"Now, what?" she asked me.

"You wait for the cops and turn yourself in," I said. "When they read you your rights or try to question you at all, you tell them you want your attorney."

"I don't have an attorney."

"Tell them it's Joel Harrity." I waited for her to repeat the name. "Like I said, he's the best in town. You talk to him and only him. He'll guide you through the rest."

"What will happen, do you think?"

"I'll leave that up to Harrity," I said. "If I had to guess, I'd say there's a chance he might have you make a statement to the detective. How much money do you think you stole?"

She considered for a few moments. "Maybe thirty-five thousand."

"So, the other two hundred thousand-plus was Rena?"

"Yes."

I spread my hands open once more. "It seems like you're the small fish in this scenario."

Laura scoffed lightly. "Lawrence will never go after Rena. Not criminally, anyway."

"Lawrence is gone," I said. "He died a few days ago."

Laura stared at me, her eyes glistening. "I'm sorry to hear that. I've been angry at him, but…"

"Just listen to what Harrity has to say," I told her. "He'll know the best strategy."

Laura nodded slowly. She opened her mouth to ask something else and stopped. Both of us heard the sound of tires on the roadway outside and the low rumble of an engine.

"The police?" Laura asked.

I motioned toward the shotgun. "You might want to set that aside now."

"Oh." She glanced down as if she'd forgotten about it. She placed it gingerly on the floor at her feet.

We stood and went to the door. As we stepped onto the porch, I saw only a single vehicle coming up the driveway. Erik's Mustang.

Laura noticed the same. She glanced down toward the driveway entrance, then my way, and crossed her arms. "You lied to me."

"No," I said. "I told you the truth."

Erik pulled to a stop. He got out of his car and closed the door, but came no closer. He only stared at Laura then looked over at me. He took a few faltering steps toward us, then paused.

"Laura…"

She didn't answer.

Erik came forward again. "I thought you were…"

Laura watched him, saying nothing.

Erik's tongue darted out to lick his lips. His eyes cut to me. "You said she might be…"

"I was wrong," I said. "Thankfully."

Erik took another few steps, halting an arm's length away. "Laura, I… I'm…"

"Did you talk to the police?" I asked him.

Erik swallowed as he nodded. "They're sending a deputy over."

"All right," I said. "Good."

Neither of them said a word. Erik stared at Laura and she stared back. I didn't try to decipher the mix of emotions hanging in the air between them. Instead, I said, "I'll give you two some space." I stepped off the porch and turned to Laura. "Can I have my phone back, please?"

Woodenly, she drew it out of her pocket and extended it toward me. I took it and walked away, stopping near the front of my car. I eased myself back onto the low hood and waited. In my peripheral vision, I saw Laura sit down on the top step of the porch. A few moments later, Erik climbed the steps and sat beside her. Neither spoke. I only glanced over at them once before the deputy arrived ten minutes later. They sat with at least a foot of space between them. Laura's arms remained crossed, as if she were hugging herself. Erik's uninjured hand dangled uselessly across his knees. Both stared off in opposite directions, implacable expressions on their faces. The image reminded me of the famous final scene of *The Graduate* as if the two of them were in the same situation as the characters in the film — lost and unsure what was to come next.

I was right there with them.

44

The next few days went by in a whirlwind of activity.

I was mostly an observer, aside from the detailed report I would eventually complete for Harrity. I watched Laura's arrest up at the cabin. The Stevens County Deputy was a veteran cop, his drooping mustache heavily streaked with iron gray with more of the same at his temples. He listened briefly to each of us, spoke to the dispatcher on the radio, and asked Laura to stand up. He put handcuffs on her without incident, searched her, and put her into the back of his Chevy Blazer.

All the while, she never spoke a word to Erik, barely even looking his direction. Since the time he sat down on the porch near her, he followed suit.

I drove back into River City and briefed Harrity. Halfway through my telling, he received a call from Laura Shelton, who'd been booked into the Stevens County Jail in Colville, an hour to the north. After a short conversation, it was clear Erik would be able to post bail for her using their home as collateral. Harrity made an appointment for her to come to his office the next day.

"What do you think will happen to her?" I asked.

Harrity pursed his lips. He didn't like to handicap his cases. For that reason, I rarely asked him to do so. On the rare occasions I did ask, he always entertained my question.

"The prosecutor will have no problems aggregating the individual instances of theft into a single scheme," he said. "The amount she stole constitutes First Degree Theft, a Class B Felony."

"That's up to ten years," I muttered. "Seems like a lot for what she did, especially since Rena stole seven times that much for three times as long."

"The actions of Ms. Pines do little to mitigate Ms. Shelton's," Harrity said. "Her intent to frame Ms. Shelton for those crimes might generate some sympathy from a jury. If a judge rules the allegation admissible, that is."

"Do you plead her guilty?" I asked.

"It's a possibility. We'll have to explore all of our options once all of the facts are on the table."

"She's a first-time offender. That ought to count for something."

"It will," Harrity agreed. "We shall see."

"Serena Pines? What will she get?"

"For embezzling money from what is now her own business?" Harrity gave me a pointed look. "Given the limited resources the prosecutor has, I am dubious any charges will be filed against her."

"So, she just gets a pass?"

Harrity spread his hands and said nothing.

I shook my head. "This fucking world," I muttered.

45

That night, Anna stopped by on her way into work. We had a light dinner and I gave her the broad strokes about what happened. I played down the confrontation with Tyler and left out entirely the fact Laura held a shotgun on me. I knew she often did the same when relaying events that happened while she was on patrol. Both of us were aware of the dangers the other faced. Neither of us needed stark reminders of it.

"Sounds like a slam dunk theft case," Anna observed, popping a small floret of broccoli into her mouth.

"It is," I agreed. "Simple." Then I thought of my first game of checkers with Mick Darabont, across the street in the park. How he characterized a simple game, one I thought was mostly for children. "And yet," I added, "not so simple."

Anna finished chewing before she spoke. Then she said, "You like her. I can tell."

I shrugged. "Like? I don't know. I feel sorry for her. I think she was a good person at her core, an otherwise happy person, until events and people just seemed to grind her down."

"Stealing tens of thousands of dollars over ten years isn't just an event. It's self-inflicted."

"You're right, though she only stole money for two years. Rena was the one doing it long term."

"She still stole," said Anna, "and had a two-year relationship with a barber. Like I said before, that doesn't sound like a happy person."

"I know. It was also a response to other stuff."

Anna turned down the corners of her mouth. "Lots of hard events happen to people who don't deserve it. I see examples almost every night. That doesn't justify stealing from your boss. Or any other crimes, for that matter."

"No, it doesn't. I don't know if it merits a decade in prison, either."

"With no previous record, she won't get anywhere near that long," Anna said, gently stabbing a pasta shell and another piece of broccoli. "She'll get three years, with two of them suspended. She'll spend maybe eight months at the county jail and she'll be out. There'll be a fine, of course, and restitution."

"Restitution," I repeated, thinking about what that word really meant. In Laura's case, it meant paying back money to the woman who intended on framing her for thefts she didn't commit. And in mine?

I pushed the thought away. Some mistakes you can never make up for. All you can do is move forward.

46

The next day, Harrity informed me Tyler Driggs was stopped by a River City patrol officer the previous evening when he ran a stop sign. He told me this just a few minutes before Laura Shelton arrived at the office for her interview.

"What does that mean?" I asked.

"I imagine it means the assault charge will move forward."

"What about his threats up at the cabin?"

"That'll be up to a different prosecutor, since they happened in Stevens County. Since all the evidence is testimonial, I doubt there will be any charges in that matter."

I shrugged, not really caring. The assault on Erik was enough to put Tyler away for years.

Laura arrived exactly on time. I half-expected her to have either Erik or Missy in tow, but she was alone. I wondered about the two of them. Would either one stay part of her life after all of this shook out? I had my doubts.

Harrity explained to Laura they would be meeting Detective Dow at one o'clock so she could

290

execute an arrest warrant and book Laura for theft. It was a formality, as she'd be immediately released on the same transferred bond Erik had previously posted with their home as collateral.

Once that was finished, Harrity turned to the interview process. "Tell me what happened," he told her. "Leave nothing out."

Laura related her story for Harrity. Overall, I learned nothing new except it was apparent the three of them hadn't yet discussed anything about the affair between Missy and Erik. I wondered if Laura would be able to forgive either one of them.

For her part, Laura didn't hold back. She shared every detail with Harrity, who listened and made meticulous notes. We took one break to refresh ourselves. During that brief time, I saw Laura standing alone, deep in thought. I watched her for a moment and remembered the light that shone out of her in the photo taken of her in the bridesmaid's dress, ready for her sister's nuptials. I hadn't seen any glimmer of that returning yet. I wished it for her though. I wished she could find that joy, become that person again. I worried her sister's and husband's betrayal might have snuffed it out forever.

When I approached, Laura's smile was forced and perfunctory.

"How are you?" I asked her.

"Making do," she said, her voice wavering.

"It's a lot to deal with," I said.

"That's an understatement."

"It will pass, though," I assured her. "Trust me."

Her expression was dubious.

"It will," I repeated. "Have you thought about what comes after? For you, I mean. When all this is done."

Laura took a deep breath and let it out while she considered my question. "I don't know. I'll have to work it out." She glanced toward the opening to Harrity's office and back to me. "From the sound of it, I'll have some considerable time alone in a jail cell to think it over."

"Hopefully not too long," I said.

"One hour is too long, if you ask me. Months… or years? I'm sure it will feel like forever."

"It will," I admitted. I spoke from personal experience, though my scant fifteen days in the county jail didn't measure up to the time Laura was facing.

"However long it is," she said, "I need to figure out how to move forward," her eyes cut briefly down to her hands, "and who is a part of that."

"You mean Erik?"

"Oh, I already know where I stand with him. But you can't divorce your sister. Truth is, I don't know if I want to, either. But I also don't know if…" she trailed off, shaking her head.

"And Ted?"

Laura laughed softly, though there was something rueful in her tone. "Ted is sweet. Maybe there's something there. Either way, I need some time to figure it out. To do what's right for me. After everything that's happened, I think I owe it to myself."

I didn't answer her. Mick Darabont's gruff voice played in my ear, his words echoing hers.

"Nobody owes anybody anything but the truth."

I wondered how much good knowing the truth was doing Laura Shelton at the moment.

"And sometimes not even that."

In the end, I supposed knowing the truth and facing it was better than the alternative. It was better than living a life full of lies, a life of illusion.

Wasn't it?

"Thanks," Laura said to me. "For your help."

I didn't know how to answer that with anything other than a nod. I wanted to add that she'd be okay, that she'd find that light in herself again, but that wasn't my promise to make. Instead, I said, "We should get back."

Laura cleared her throat. "Sure," she said. "I'm ready."

Back in Harrity's office, we picked up the process where we'd left off. By the time Laura finished, it was nearly noon. As usual, Harrity had listened with rapt attention. He asked insightful questions, drew out small facts I knew would matter later on whether he was negotiating with the prosecutor or working the case in the courtroom.

"Is there anything more you have to share with me?" he finally asked Laura.

Laura Shelton shook her head. "I've told you everything I know," she said.

Her expression was weary, but a shade brighter than it had been even earlier in the day. No, perhaps not *brighter* exactly, but certainly lighter. Maybe it was getting to tell her story that took some of the weight from her shoulders. Confession was supposedly good for the soul.

"Very well," Harrity said. He stood and I followed suit. "I believe the detective is waiting for us," he said.

Laura hesitated a moment, staring ahead at nothing in particular, as if gathering her resolve. Then she, too, stood, forcing a half-confident smile.

"Time to face the future," she said.

Then, together, we left the office to take her to be arrested.

Acknowledgments

I'd like to thank:

Colin Conway, for pointing out the two biggest flaws in an early draft.

Kelli Peacock, for offering some accounting insight.

Beta readers Paula Dunn, Gary Felix, Suzanne Peckham, John Emery, Sue Bryson, Dave Mather, Kim Erickson, Ron Sarich, Barb Stoner and Jiver Freecloud.

And Kristi, for helping me find the truest Laura.

Frank Zafiro
April 2024
Redmond, Oregon

About the Author

Frank Zafiro writes gritty crime fiction written from both sides of the badge.

He was a police officer from 1993 to 2013, where he worked patrol, investigations, commanded K9 and SWAT, and retired as a captain.

An award-winning author, Frank has written more than fifty books, including his River City series, and collaborated with five different authors, including Colin Conway and Eric Beetner. As Frank Scalise, he writes family drama, humorous and heartwarming novels, and children's and middle grade sports novels. As Frank Saverio, he writes science fiction and fantasy.

In addition to writing, Frank hosts the podcast *Wrong Place, Write Crime.* He is an avid hockey fan and a tortured guitarist. He lives in Redmond, Oregon.

You can keep up with him at http://frankzafiro.com.